THE INFLUENCER

THE INFLUENCER

Adriane Leigh

THE INFLUENCER

Adriane Leigh

Praise for The Influencer

"What a wild ride!"

"Intense. Addicting. Toxically diabolical."

"Addicting and toxic. Absolutely phenomenal from start to finish. I couldn't put this one down."

"A psychological thrill ride. Hello *Mr. Ripley!* A slow journey into obsession. Dark, twisted, and great for mystery fans."

"Wow! What did I just read!!?? Had me flipping the pages right to the spectacular, mindblowing, I-didn't-see-that-coming ending!"

Epigraph

Innocence, Once Lost, Can Never Be Regained.
Darkness, Once Gazed Upon, Can Never Be Lost.

-John Milton

Prologue

My lungs balloon painfully in my chest.

I can't breathe. I can't breathe. I can't breathe.

The last spasms of life rack my body as my mouth fights to contain the scream in my throat. My limbs thrash as my eyes search the murky dark waters for anything to grasp on to.

This is it.

And I never saw it coming.

The bitch fooled me, and the knowledge of that chills my veins even more than the glacially cold waters.

I can't breathe. I can't breathe. I can't breathe.

I blink away the shadows as the waters mix with my tears. My future has been extinguished. Now, what's left of me will be found in a heap of forgotten trash in the heart of the city.

Darkness. Drowning. Dying.

I sob, wishing for the warmth of Dean's arms around me just one last time.

And then my world fades to black.

Chapter One

A few months ago...

Brunch with a view at @ThePoloLounge then cocktails at @ThePalm later! #blessed

My fingers speed across the screen as I type out the caption and then hit post on the Instagram photo. It's a closely cropped shot of my mimosa. The two-carat canary diamond ring Dean gifted me for our last anniversary is centered in the shot, glittering from my ring finger as I hold the stem of the champagne flute. The morning sun casts a halo effect of golden perfection in the background, and I know my followers will love it. I love my life—or at least, the one my followers think I have. To them, I am Mia Starr, Hollywood Hills native, and living the life they've always dreamed of. Being chic and fabulous is my brand, even if it isn't exactly true-to-life.

The truth is, my life *is* perfect *most* of the time.

I have a great house; it's just not in Beverly Hills. I have a wonderful, faceless husband who has made my wildest dreams come true. From the gutter to the red carpet, that's the narrative I present when I log in each day. People love an underdog story.

I scroll my newsfeed, countless smiling faces peering back at me, all fake teeth and fake diamonds and living their own version of happily-ever-after. I know, on some level, I'm tricking them. But aren't we all? Social media presents the perfect opportunity to live the life you've always dreamed of, at least in the eyes of the ones who matter. To them, Mia Starr has everything. In real life, Shae Halston is a struggling train wreck with enough family baggage to fill a jetliner and more debt than a developing nation.

Dean is in the high-end real estate business, and while he's made a great career for himself, our life in California is only getting more expensive. It doesn't help that my job doesn't really profit—I'm successful as far as influencers go. I'm approaching 100,000 followers on Instagram—my favorite social media app—but monetizing my following has been difficult, to say the least. I have a flourishing website, but selling pdf files and cheap custom-designed jewelry doesn't exactly pay the bills. It's Dean's business deals that provide the life I've always dreamed of. Recently, advertisers have taken notice and are eager to send me free products to gush to my followers about. And sometimes, if I'm lucky, they pay me a small commission on every sale. But overall, Mia Starr is a brand, not a person. She's a facade, and I'm not even the face.

I began this venture out of boredom, sharing restaurant and product reviews with what's become known as my characteristic wit. I represent the good life to people, and so I leaned in. I grew to more than 25,000 followers in a few short months, and it was then I realized that to continue to scale, I'd need a face for Mia Starr. I didn't want to share my own face; the family I'd worked so hard to escape would be at my doorstep in a moment if they knew I was the brains behind the brand that was constantly recommended on their social feeds. Plus, I liked being someone new. Shae Halston had baggage. Mia Starr is a star in the making. Glamorous, poised, elegant, everything I'd spent so much time envying.

When Dean suggested we use a modeling agency to find the perfect face to represent Mia, I agreed eagerly, only a little embarrassed I hadn't thought of the idea myself. Within twenty-four hours, we were sifting through headshots and discussing which platinum blonde would help me grow what had become a quickly expanding social media brand. Choosing a blonde made sense. I could be in some of the photos. My blond waves would be easily interchangeable with the model's in obscure shots at the beach or from behind at elegant restaurants and trendy clubs—but the full-face photos were always a model. It seemed so simple at the time, and when Jesika Layman's sparkling blue eyes shone from her headshot that first day, we knew she was the one.

Dean hummed that she looked like me, the same dip in her nose and similar full pink lips. I knew he was trying to flatter me, but I liked being flattered. We hired Jesika on the spot for a custom photo shoot with the agency's preferred photographer. Within two weeks, I had a file in my inbox with dozens of shots from the photo shoot, some taken outside in the sunshine, some poolside, others at chic outdoor eateries, sparkling champagne in hand as she laughed at someone off-camera.

She was perfect. She was me, but better. She was my Mia.

Chapter Two

Soaking up the sun! I caption the video on my profile, adding a sun emoji as an afterthought before uploading it to my private profile story. My followers love when I include them in moments from my daily life, and I artfully position the video to avoid the run-down El Segundo Beach sign that's just out of the shot. The wild inconsistency between the perfection of Hollywood and the dilapidation of El Segundo, with its crumbling sidewalks and rusted street signs, is like a metaphor for my life. Like a persistent weed growing between the cement slabs of the boulevard, I refuse to be snuffed out. Talent and charm have gotten me this far, but only dogged determination will take me further.

The cab driver slows at a stop sign before turning onto the street that will deliver me to the condo Dean and I live in. Normally, we live in the recently renovated homes that dot the Hollywood Hills or the mountains of Malibu before Dean sells them to the highest bidder—but real estate has slowed the last few months, and Dean is struggling to compete in a market where even the fixer-uppers are priced in the multimillions. He's resorted to turning to bank loans to fund the last few projects. But affording the posh furnishings and luxury details his clients expect are eating up our profit quicker than it used to, so the bank isn't willing to extend him the same line of credit they once did. I'm not worried. Dean is a hustler and always has been; it's just one of the things I love about him. I know we'll weather this temporary storm in our finances, but that's why I'm so focused on taking Mia to the next level. This needs to work out for us. Otherwise, we'll be moving out of El Segundo and be forced farther away from the coast—and the California coast is my brand.

I can't afford the cab rides to Beverly Hills every day, so I've resorted to biweekly trips where I spend all day snapping photos and taking videos for behind-the-scenes stories and then doling them out over the course of the next two weeks, as if I'm spending every day floating around the chicest LA hot spots. It's not ideal, but so far, my followers haven't noticed that anything is off. That's the thing about social media. You can be whoever you want with a little extra filtering and some motivation. I've even taken to shopping the luxury stores on Robertson, snapping photos as I try on designer heels or handbags as if I'm buying the items, when really, it's just glorified window-shopping. When Dean and I actually go out for dinner, I've been known to buy a thousand-dollar designer dress and tuck the tags inside the zipper for the night before returning it the following morning.

It hasn't always been this way. When Dean and I were dating and his houses were turning a multimillion-dollar profit, he bought me enough dresses to fill our walk-in closet, but I can't be photographed in the same dress twice. Practical fashion isn't my brand. Sophisticated luxury is.

The cab slows, and the driver frowns when I slide my credit card into the card reader. I know he'd rather I pay in cash, but cash is at a premium for us at the moment, and my line of credit is quickly dwindling. I've taken to reaching out to potential advertisers and offering a discount on my typical commission in an effort to lure them into sending me more products to sample.

I'm lucky to be in the position I'm in, but being Mia Starr doesn't come cheap.

"Thank you," I say to the annoyed cab driver as I step out of the cracked back seat. Mia would have a private driver or take an Uber at the very least, but I'm making do—sharing my content in a fresh way that cleverly overlooks the fact that our lifestyle isn't what it once was. Dean has been under a lot of stress, and I've spent the last year escaping into Mia's life. I even joke with Dean sometimes and ask, *What would Mia do?*

He always scoffs and rolls his eyes like my brand is only a little hobby. And maybe it once was, but as soon as we had Jesika's face in our back pocket, the follower count grew exponentially. Authenticity reigns in a world of online scammers and social media fake filters, and I've done everything I can to lean into that. Dean has withdrawn more over the months, distancing himself from all that Mia Starr is, but she's become my everything. My reason for waking up in the morning and putting one foot in front of the other when it feels like everything else in our lives is falling apart.

Stepping into the condo, I can tell Dean is home already. He isn't usually home from the office until late evening, often taking clients out to dinner or scheduling meetings for later in the day with contractors, so it's unusual that I can hear the low murmur of his voice on a phone call. A smile turns up my lips as I kick off my Fendi slides and move through the rooms in search of him. By the time I find him, I realize there's a reason he's home early, and it's not good.

"I think it's time we call this, Shae."

He doesn't smile when I step into his office. He hasn't smiled for a while when we've greeted each other after a long day. In fact, he's been sleeping on the sofa in his office more nights than not, but I like to assume it's because he's working late. Not because of me.

"What do you mean?" I settle myself in the armchair opposite his desk and sigh.

"Sign these. I've been generous."

"Generous?" My eyes cut to the paperwork he's sliding across the polished mahogany. "Generous about what?"

My husband presses his lips together and tosses a pen onto the stack of papers. "I kept everything simple, straightforward. You can hire a lawyer if you want, but you're entitled to fifty percent of everything I earned while we were together."

"What?" Fear bubbles up inside me.

"We've been headed in this direction for a while, you know we have. Please don't make it more difficult by acting blindsided."

"Dean…" I can't look at the paperwork. I can only hold his hardened gaze. "Please," I beg. "Is this about her?" I finally ask, my tone accusatory.

"Of course not."

I grit my teeth. He averts his eyes to the window that overlooks the street below us. I have the sudden urge to throw something at his head, but I temper my rage. For now.

"Please, just sign them."

I'm fuming. My fingers shake as I pick up the pen, and instead of signing the divorce papers like he's asking, I whip it at his head. "I won't do it."

"Shae, for chrissakes, it doesn't matter if you sign them. California is a no-fault state. The judge will grant me the divorce, and I'm giving you half of everything I have."

"You don't have anything to give, you asshole!"

Dean only shrugs. "I gave you a good life."

"Until you started fucking other people." I'm seething, and suddenly, I wish he were dead.

He only rolls his eyes. "Listen, I understand you're hurt, but you knew I was like this. We met while I was still married to Denise. Come on, you knew who I was. I never tried to hide anything from you."

"So...so, I should have seen this coming? I thought you loved me."

"I did. Of course I loved you. I still do."

Tears burn at my eyelids. He's the closest thing to love I've ever felt.

"I did the best I could by you, Shae. But come on, you know things haven't been the same since she came into our lives."

I know by *she*, he means Mia Starr, my online persona. He's been constantly annoyed by how much time I spend in *La-La Land,* as he calls it. When we're at dinner, he grumbles when I ask him to take a photo of me, revealing just enough to make it authentic without revealing so much that followers recognize that I am not who they think I am. He thinks I've become obsessed. I think he's jealous of the attention I'm receiving. We agreed to disagree over this long ago, but apparently Dean has come to some decisions all on his own.

"I'm leaving tonight. I'd like to drop the papers off with the attorney in the morning, but I'm gonna need you to sign them first."

Dejected, I grit my teeth and take the new pen he's offering me. "Did you tell the attorney you're fucking someone else?"

"It's not relevant. We don't have kids, our savings has dwindled to nothing, and we cashed out our long-term investments last year to float the mortgage on the Nichols Canyon bungalow before it sold. Give it a look-over. I have time. I can wait."

"Are you going to her place tonight?" I whip the second pen at his head.

"It's not your business."

"I-I thought we had an understanding? If I overlooked your slutty ways—"

"Don't start this, Shae. Please. You have your own life, I have mine. We've been living separately for a while. This just finalizes it."

I'm fuming at the audacity of his trying to talk me down after everything we've been through. Although, he's right. I can't fault him for leaving me for another woman. It's the same thing he did to his first wife. Dean isn't the kind of man that gets along alone very well—of course he had someone else lined up to take my place.

"I can't believe I let you fool me for this long. I should have left when I found the hotel receipts for the weekend in Santa Barbara. I should have left and taken you for everything then—"

His laugh is meant to infuriate me. He shakes his head. "There was no everything. Not even then. You've been burning through my profits as quickly as I can make them, to support Mia."

"I can't believe I fell for a snake like you," I seethe, grasping the only thing within my reach, a stupid glass-and-gold award Dean won for being the top seller at the first real estate agency he worked with when he moved to Los Angeles. I chuck it as hard as I can at his head, and he ducks, narrowly missing the edge of the plaque before it shatters the window behind his head and lands with a thunk on the street below.

"Don't you fucking dare, Shae Miller." I cringe when he uses my maiden name. The name I've been trying to kill since the day we met.

"Watch me." I swipe a coffee table book of Malibu beach homes from the desk and chuck it at him. He shields his face with his forearm, and the hardcover drops to the floor, spine splitting. He's on me then, clutching both of my wrists and shoving me against the broken window. My heart jackhammers inside my chest as I realize he could end me here. He's towering over me, using all his strength to keep my petite form from attacking him. I'd kill him right now if I thought I could get away with it. My mind flashes to how I'll explain this to my followers. Divorce doesn't fit into the narrative of Mia's life.

"Fuck with me, and I will ruin you where it counts, Shae."

"Drop dead," I boil.

His eyes round and his nostrils flare before he cocks his arm back and slaps me hard across the face. Tears sting my eyes, and I can feel a sharp tingle where his palm will leave a mark on my cheek.

"I'll expose Mia as a fraud to your followers, Shae. If you so much as whisper a word in my direction again, I'll expose you to everyone."

Fury instantly possesses me. The kind of fury that makes me a stranger in my own skin. The calm that usually inhabits me takes flight, and in its place, unbridled malevolence fills every throbbing fiber of my frame. "You wouldn't."

We worked so hard to build Mia Starr. He could tear me down with a few finger swipes. But would he?

As if he can read my mind, he says, "I would in a fucking heartbeat."

And suddenly, years of love are forgotten in the hatred of a single moment.

Chapter Three

My bloodstream vibrates with red wine as I swipe aimlessly through my newsfeed. While chic shots of faraway places and designer attire would normally distract me, now they're only working the sadness deeper into my muscles. My body aches with the profound sense of loss I'm feeling. I know Dean isn't a good man, but I thought he was good for me. I thought we were good together. Love is like that sometimes. I was never looking for a knight in shining armor; I was only looking for someone to fill the cracks that webbed across my heart from years of neglect. I know I'll be fine. I know I'll overcome the bump in the road that is my ruined marriage. But I'm not sure Mia will. My entire persona is predicated on wealth and luxury, the life Dean and I built together. I can still visit high-end designers and snap try-on photos, but it will be harder, so much harder. Dean's access to the real estate world afforded him invites to luxury mansions and chic private lounges where I could sip champagne and pretend that my life is perfect.

Now, pretending will take much more planning.

I type Jesika Layman's name into my search bar, and her

profile pops up instantly. She's the top name in my search. I don't follow her, because that would clue my followers in to the face behind the facade, but I do check out her profile at least weekly. From New York to London to Ibiza, she has the life I've been pretending to have. While I know the reality of a working model isn't as glamorous as it seems, it's leaps and bounds more glam than mine.

Her most recent picture is tagged at the Polo Lounge, and I balk. It wouldn't be the end of the world if we ran into each other in real life. She's never seen me and wouldn't recognize the features of my plain Jane face. The thought occurs to me that maybe she has been recognized as Mia Starr, though. I frown, figuring she would chalk it up to a case of a doppelgänger and then move on with her day. Or maybe she knows she's the face of a personal brand. But Dean and I paid top dollar for the photo shoot and photos, and we even had her and the agency sign a nondisclosure regarding how the photos would be used. It must be weird. Being a model makes her a professional at becoming someone else. A familiar face without an identity. A beautiful liar.

I slide down her profile to the last week of photos, and I notice a pattern. She's in LA right now—that much is obvious because she's quick to tag herself wherever she goes—but she's also visiting locations Dean liked to take me to. My heart thrums wildly as I continue to scroll until I reach a well-posed photo of her on the beach with a mystery man.

Sunsets with my baby are my favorite! xo

I pinch the screen with my fingers and zoom in on the arm that's causally wrapped around her shoulders. One hand—clearly a man's—is in the shot, the thick knuckles dusted with dark hair and one gleaming platinum ring.

I gasp in disbelief.

I know that ring. The intricate web of filigree that wraps

around the gem mounted in the center would be recognizable anywhere. It's the ring Dean received from the Los Angeles Board of Realtors when he outsold everyone else at his agency his first year working for them. He profited nearly half a billion for the company that first year, his smooth-talking charm sealing countless deals as he hustled his way through Malibu, Santa Monica, and the Hollywood Hills.

The year we met.

I hated that ring and teased him about it endlessly. It's gaudy and ostentatious and, for me, only represented his dedication to making the company rich and not us. His commission was abysmal that year because he was a freshman agent, and it was because of that that I convinced him to strike out on his own and build his own company. He was born with natural charm, and after that first year, he'd garnered enough networking connections to turn all of his hard work into sales. I believed in him, I still do, and after months of my convincing, he finally submitted his resignation to the company and started his own real estate agency. He was the singular agent, with me at his side to help seal the deals, but the stars never aligned for us. The agency seemed dead on arrival, and while we had a few good years, we struggled to keep the company afloat even in the best of times. The truth of it was, that despite all of Dean's charm, neither of us had a head for finances and business management. I can't help but feel regret now, wondering where we'd be if he'd stayed with the company that had brought him so much success initially. I should have kept my mouth shut on the matter, because opening my mouth had hastened the end of us. And that ring gave me a wicked sense of PTSD as a result.

I scroll deeper into Jesika's archive of photos, going back weeks and months in search of more shots of her mystery man. I find only one more, three months ago at a club in Brooklyn. She captioned the photo: **Girls' night out + a surprise drop-in from my favorite guy!**

I cringe as I take in the photo. Three glasses of bubbly champagne toasting and a single glass of whisky. I imagine that it's Dean's favorite, Macallan. And again, there is the ring. Tears prick my eyelids as I realize what this means.

Dean has been cheating on me with my doppelgänger. My online persona. He's fallen for the pretend me.

And I hate him for it. How could he be so cruel?

I think back to the day we sorted through headshots on the modeling agency's website. How after dozens of girls, he'd singled one out. Her sleek, silver-blond hair and striking blue eyes struck him. It was because of his enthusiasm for that particular model that I'd chosen her. When we'd visited the modeling agency and signed the documents, he'd insisted on handling the paperwork. Now I know why. *He'd* chosen her, not us. He'd managed to replace me right in front of my own eyes. That was over a year ago, just about the time he'd grown distant and started spending more time at work and passing out on the sofa in his office instead of coming to our marriage bed.

I grit my teeth, killing the app before emptying the rest of the bottle of red wine into my glass. I finish the remainder in one swallow, the bitter sediment settled at the bottom of the glass causing me to cringe. I imagine posting hateful comments on her profile photos, calling her a home-wrecker or worse—a worthless, opportunistic whore—but then I realize it would be no better than name-calling myself. After all, isn't that what I'd done? Found a successful man and uprooted him from his life and marriage for my own selfish benefit?

I hate her, but I hate him more.

I open the app again, wine settling like a thick fog in my mind as I view my own profile, Jesika's smiling face beaming at the lens every handful of posts under the guise of Mia. On impulse, and with the urge to take control of the narrative of my life, I snap a candid shot of the wine bottle and my hand holding the empty wineglass. Without thinking, I type in the only caption that's running through my head on a painful loop: **My husband is dead to me.**

I hit submit on the post, tears welling in my eyes as I realize I'll have a lot of explaining to do in the morning, but right now, I only want to sleep. Tomorrow is a new day. Tomorrow, I'll deal with the fallout. But tonight, I'll let bitter tears stain my cheeks until I fall asleep.

Chapter Four

I'm pulled from my sweet sleep escape by the sound of notifications buzzing on my phone. With a groan, I roll over and swipe it off the coffee table. My back aches from sleeping on the couch, and the morning sun is splitting through the living room curtains, causing the slow throb of a headache to start behind my frontal lobe.

With sleep in my eyes, I glance at the screen of my cell and frown.

Praying for you.
Sending love.
RIP 🩶

"What?" I murmur into the empty space. I swipe to open the Instagram app, but my phone instantly dies. In the haze of wine and heartache, I forgot to charge the battery. I groan, shooting off the couch and beelining for my Gucci bucket bag in the kitchen. I dig through the piles of my broken life in search of my charger, and when I find it, I shove it into the kitchen socket and plug in my phone and wait.

I could use a coffee. Normally, Dean would have had a freshly brewed pot waiting for me, but now I'm on my own.

What in the hell did I post last night that has garnered that kind of response?

Once the phone powers on, a hundred more notifications buzz to life. I have an inbox full of messages, and based on the comments, my post with the wine bottle and glass has apparently gone viral. I open the app quickly and swipe to my last post.

And then horror settles into my bones.

My caption from last night reads: **My husband is dead**

That's it. I'd meant to post *dead to me*, but in my wine-soaked haze, my brain must've left off the rest of the caption. And as soon as I'd hit submit, I'd put down my phone and fallen asleep, eager to forget the last few hours of yesterday.

And now my followers think my husband is dead.

In all honesty, he is—*to me*.

As I rub my palms over my eyes, thoughts shuttle through my mind while I consider what steps to take next. Come clean? Tell them it was a drunken thumb-slip? Embarrassment colors my face as the shame of my mistake descends on me.

I scroll down through the comments. More than a thousand people are praying for me and wishing me well. One follower has even set up a GoFundMe page for funeral expenses.

"Oh. Dear. God."

I can't even begin to process how to undo the damage from this errant caption. I click over to the donation page link that my follower has posted and see that more than three hundred people have already donated more than five thousand dollars, and the donations are coming in fast. As I linger on the page, the live ticker of money received is moving up.

My heart sinks.

And then I think that the money could help with living expenses—after all, Dean has left me nothing. There is nothing to leave, and my brand relies more on free gifts than it does actual cash. The truth remains; Dean *is* dead to me. And if I don't figure out something fast, I'll be on the streets. I add too much value to the daily lives of my followers to let that happen. And I have been mourning a death—only it's the death of my marriage, not an actual, physical death.

The heart inside my chest cavity burns as I consider what it would mean if I actually keep the money and continue this ruse. Can I do it? Would anyone know the difference? I imagine the all-black Oscar de la Renta gown I purchased for my engagement photos years ago. I could post a selfie wearing that—heck, maybe even visit the local cemetery while I do it for good measure and share it with my followers. I imagine the viral sensation it would cause and probably make me even more money. After all, people love to support a cause, and I have been sharing quality content in the way of inspiring captions to brighten all of their feeds day after day for years.

I deserve this.

The more I think about it, the more I realize this isn't a bump in the road of my career. I'll only have to pivot the tone of my content for a while as I mourn the loss. My blood hums with energy as I begin to strategize my way out of this small snafu. And I can. I'm the master of the pivot. I managed to pivot Dean away from his wife, his lucrative career... I can do this. And it will only be temporary. Just long enough to get back on my feet and get that online life-coaching element of my brand off the ground.

I log in to my email inbox, hoping to find something from that advertiser offering a commission. But instead, I find something better. I find that my Patreon page has exploded with new subscribers. For $10 a month, my subscribers get extra content like shopping lists and exclusive get-ready-with-me videos and product reviews. Before now, I was struggling to make a few hundred dollars off the Patreon each month. But overnight, my subscribers have ballooned to eight hundred people. I gasp, realizing that's $8,000 I'll make per month, as long as they remain subscribed. It's easier to keep the subscribers you have than generate new ones, and these people have fallen into my lap. I just needed a little tragedy to motivate them to support me.

Relief loosens my tense muscles as I realize I'll be okay. Thanks to these good Samaritans, I don't need Dean's money. I may not be able to afford the fancy shopping sprees anymore—that Oscar de la Renta gown was more than $8,000 alone—but I've already adapted to living a luxe life on a budget, thanks to Dean's failing business.

My soon-to-be-ex may have thrown me an entire truck of sour lemons yesterday, but my followers have helped me turn them into the sweetest lemonade. Death has given me life. Gratitude overwhelms me, and with a smile, I log in to my bank account and already find thousands of dollars pending deposit. It's like the darkness that weighed me down previously is illuminated. I feel free of the burden of my marriage, unchained from the stigma of divorce. I am a widow, as simple as that.

I think I'll take myself out to coffee this morning to celebrate my newfound success. I am the master of the pivot after all. Now, I'll just have to brainstorm a few posts to keep the lie alive for a while longer, and then I can move on with my life.

Mia Starr's husband is dead, and I couldn't be happier.

Chapter Five

72 hours.

It's been 72 hours since cancer stole the love of my life. My heart breaks with every breath. To my husband: thank you for loving me enough to finally love myself. Thank you for teaching me that love is loss and that nothing in this world is permanent. Loving you was worth the pain of losing you. I know we'll meet again some-day, my love. RIP.

I spend a minute rereading the carefully curated caption. It's emotional yet full of gratitude. I think it hits just the right note for my followers. I've been in a suspended state of grieving —or at least, I've been trying to pretend to be. And I don't have to pretend very hard. I *am* grieving the loss of my marriage. I'm grieving the loss of a relationship with a narcissistic bastard who traded me in for someone younger, fresher, more beautiful than I ever was. A model, of all things. I could never compete with her.

I sigh as I swipe through the photos I took this morning at the cemetery. The elegant black Oscar de la Renta gown strikes just the right tone. My favorite shot is one from behind. The full skirt falls in waves of taffeta from my waist, and a black lace veil cascades down my back and hides my face. I look like a mafia widow. It's dramatic. But then, everything in my life is, so why go understated now? I will grieve the loss of this man for the rest of my life and will do anything to prevent this pain from seeping into my bloodstream again.

It doesn't help that the bastard reached out to me after my first post three days ago. I knew he followed me on social media. I should have blocked him the moment he walked out the door, but in my defense, I had no idea one mistyped caption would cause my life to implode like it has. Dean didn't even seem mad about the post—he'd only text messaged me with a screenshot of my post of the wine bottle and added a simple *Don't forget to claim these donations as assets in the divorce LOL.*

I didn't answer him, but I did immediately block him from seeing anything else. That won't stop him from creating a new account if he wants to, but I don't think he would do something like that. Dean has a habit of mostly avoiding confrontation until he can't anymore. I have a feeling he's just glad to have me out of his life. He was looking to the future, and so was I. I just had to get over this mourning phase, and then I could use my expanding following to further maximize profit. I could even talk to the financial manager Dean used and ask him to invest my money so that one day I could actually retire off this gig. Dean may have left me, but I'm not about to ruin my financial future on top of everything else.

I suck in a ragged breath and then hit submit on the post before killing the app and tossing my phone onto the couch next to me. The glass guy is due in an hour to fix the gaping hole that now exists in the window in Dean's office. Opening my laptop, I type *rare forms of cancer* into the search bar and begin my research into the disease that stole my husband from me. I don't know that I will ever share details—after all, it isn't really anyone's business, but I want to have something at the ready just in case.

The first cancer listed in the search results is leukemia, but the more I read, the more it seems to be a slow-growing disease and not the right choice for my situation. I've also never known anyone who's had leukemia, so after a few minutes, I realize it might be easier if I choose something I at least have some experience with. I frown, reaching for the bottle of white wine I've already opened even though it's hardly noon and pour myself half a glass. I sip it slowly and let my mind wander through all the diseases that've afflicted my family.

While I hadn't known my grandma because she'd died before I was born, I vaguely remember my mom talking about her own mother's swift and surprising passing from an aggressive and novel form of throat cancer. She smoked like a chimney and was miserable to boot, if I was to take my mother's word for it, but regardless, my mother was rocked by the early loss of her own mom. I type *rare and aggressive forms of throat cancer* into the search bar and began reading. Dean had a love for good whisky and enjoyed the occasional cigar. Maybe I could weave that into the narrative of his passing, and it would work as a sort of cautionary tale. The more I consider this possibility, the more it seems to fit. Throat cancers are hard to diagnose early enough to treat effectively. By the time most people begin to experience symptoms, it's often grown to an unmanageable stage. Chemotherapy and radiation may help to slow the growth of tumors, but after initial treatment, the tumors often come back with a vengeance. It's perfect. Just the kind of affliction I need to corroborate my story.

If it ever comes up, I will explain that my dear, sweet Dean went from diagnosis to aggressive treatment to dead in under ninety days.

Shutting the laptop and feeling a sense of satisfaction overtake my system, I smile as I think about the caption I will post explaining my husband's swift illness and passing. I will mention that I tried to keep it under wraps because my brand is focused on positivity and uplifting content, but life isn't always a parade and I finally decided that honesty and authenticity are more important than putting on a fake smile to get through the day. I can just imagine the outpouring of love and comfort that will come from my being real with my followers, cementing them to me in a genuine and messy way. I could even make a post about the medical expenses sucking up all of our savings and retirement, and maybe that would boost the GoFundMe and Patreon donations.

A quick *knock-knock-knock* shakes me from my thoughts, and I jump off the couch, spilling white wine in my lap as I do. I cross to the front door, a very sad piece of myself hoping it's Dean back to beg for my forgiveness, but then I hear Charlie, the corgi from next door, bark, and I know it must be Margaret. The little old lady has lived next door to us since we moved in to this condo, and Charlie, sweet as he is, has kept us up many a night with his barking. I hated that dog at one point, but we made friends pretty quickly when Dean suggested that Charlie only needed to get his energy out.

So, about a year ago, I took matters into my own hands and introduced myself to Margaret, explained I was a dog lover and grew up with a corgi named Gizmo and I missed him every day —the best dog I ever had. I told her Dean was allergic so getting our own dog was out of the question, but that I'd love to walk Charlie whenever she needed, to fill the hole in my heart left by Gizmo. Margaret, I'd learned, walked with a cane and had her groceries delivered. She took me up on my offer to walk her dog and even offered to pay me, but I told her I wouldn't accept payment, that spending time with Charlie would be enough.

And so, I'd taken to walking Charlie at least a few times a week—whenever his barking got so loud it made me want to pull my hair out. The truth? There was no Gizmo, and I'd never owned a corgi and never would. Their high energy and constant need for attention drove me to the brink of insanity. Margaret was always so grateful when I brought him home and gushed what a good boy he'd been, and she always reported that I was a dog whisperer because he was always calm for a few days after our walks.

Another truth? I'd taken to drugging the poor mutt into submission. Walking him was a chore because he'd never been formally leash-trained. And so, Charlie and I walked the beach, and on the way home, I usually made a point to stop at the pet store and buy him some soft treats, his favorites. When we got back home, I pulled apart a few capsules of Benadryl and mixed them up with the treats and then let him eat to his heart's content. Charlie was always dragging when I brought him home to Margaret, too tired to move a muscle, much less bark. I was good for Charlie—if it weren't for me, he'd never get a walk—and I was practically the martyr of our small condo community because his barking ceased for at least a few days after we had our outings.

Charlie barked again, and I had half a mind to hide out but then figured a little walk would be good for both of us. Especially if I wanted some peace over the next few days.

I swung the door wide and plastered on a fake smile. "Margaret, it's good to see you."

"Hello, honey. I hate to ask, but a friend is picking me up for my physical therapy appointment in a little while, and I just know if I leave Charlie at home, he'll bark until he's hoarse and drive everyone crazy. Would you be willing to watch him for an hour or two?"

"I would love to!"

Chapter Six

"Charlie!" A shriek bleats past my lips as the dog practically yanks my shoulder out of its socket. I yank right back, anger sizzling through my veins as I imagine dropping him off at the animal shelter and being done with this menace once and for all.

Instead, I plop onto a wooden bench next to the boardwalk and force Charlie to sit at my feet. We've only been walking for five minutes. I know he must be excited since I'm the only one who walks him, but I'm distracted at best. Anxiety has my muscles bunching and aching under the stress. I shouldn't have offered to watch Charlie. I'm hardly competent enough to manage my own life, much less take care of a dog.

I sigh, wishing I could drop him off at home and get some peace, but I know he'll just start barking incessantly if I do. A jogger with a Great Dane passes us, and Charlie makes a lunge for it. He's stronger than me this time, and the leash escapes my grip. Tail wagging, he reaches the other dog that towers over him, and then he begins to bark and bounce excitedly. He's cute, but the other dog wants nothing to do with it.

"I'm sorry, he's crazy today." I offer in the way of an apology to the owner. The woman is athletic. High-end workout gear fits her lean muscles to a tee, and the pieces look fresh off the rack. I can't help the bubble of jealousy that rises within me. She's pretty, the kind of pretty that makes mediocre girls like me uncomfortable. And now she's just staring at me, like I've single-handedly ruined her day. Well, it's not my fault. It's the dog.

"Sorry again." I wave as I swipe at his leash and yank him back to the bench with me. I sit down again, careful to grip the leash with a little more strength this time as a sense of defeat overtakes me. I feel like a loser who couldn't keep her husband, but then, Dean was always a cheater. He cheated on his first wife *with me.* I should have seen this one coming, but I was too busy with my own life to even consider the full extent of what he might be up to in his free time.

In an effort to distract myself, I pull out my phone and check my notifications in Instagram. The outpouring of sympathy and messages of support send a grateful tingle through my system. I smile as I heart a few of the comments, type out a few quick *thank yous,* and then jump to my newsfeed and begin to scroll. As if the algorithm knows how to hit below the belt, the first photo that loads is of *her.*

Jesika.

The model. *My model.* My Mia.

My stomach burns with bitterness as I realize what she's announcing to her followers. Her photo is carefully curated, a testing stick with two pink lines held in her left hand...and on her left ring finger? A princess cut diamond with double rows of pavé cut stones wrapping around the band.

She's pregnant and engaged. *To my husband.* I feel like I want to die.

So this is why he did it. It's been less than a week since he walked away from me, and it's because of this. Because of her.

Because they have a secret. Well, it's not so much a secret anymore. Once it's social-media official, there's no take backs.

I hate him. I hate her. I hate everything about this, including myself. I hate that I trusted him and he made a fool out of me.

"Come on, you fucking mutt," I mutter, standing from the bench and pulling Charlie along with me. He senses my energy and follows a few steps behind me, as if he's scared of what I might do next. Well, he should be. Anger is stirring inside me. All I can think about is getting revenge and ruining their lives like they've ruined mine.

Within a few minutes, we're back at the condo. Charlie veers to Margaret's front door to go home, but I pull him back on the path to mine. A thousand emotions are swirling through my head. Like, how long have they known? When did they start dating? Does she realize who he is? Suddenly, I think I should block her on my social media if she does. The last thing I need is to log in and find some shitty comment from her on one of my posts. But then, if I block her, I lose the small window I have into their life. I'm not ready for that. Sure, it might be the healthier decision, but I'm not ready for healthy yet.

I'm ready for revenge.

Once we're in the condo, I unhook Charlie's leash, and he looks up at me and wags his tail.

"Good boy. I'm sorry our walk was short today." I pat him on the head. "Do you want a treat?" With that, his little ears twitch, and he wags his tail. "Just give me a minute, Char."

My mind still swirling with anger and pain, I slide over to the fridge and open it, eyes searching for something to give Charlie. I pull out a pack of thawed ground hamburger and open the corner. I tear off a piece and toss it at Charlie, and he eats it eagerly, then comes closer and asks for more with his big brown puppy-dog eyes.

He's a cutie. I can see why he's a good companion for a little old lady. I just wish he were a little calmer and quieter. I toss Charlie another small chunk of meat and then open the medicine drawer to grab the Benadryl I use to give him a little more chill than he was born with. I frown when I realize the bottle is empty. Just one more thing Dean left me to deal with, I guess. I head back to the cabinet and search for something else to do the trick. In the way back, I find liquid Benadryl from when Dean had strep last year and couldn't sleep at night. He couldn't swallow pills, his throat was so swollen and painful, so he'd sent me to the store for the liquid version.

I uncap it, scan the dosage instructions on the back, then pull a small bowl from the cupboard and toss some ground beef into the dish, dumping some of the liquid on top. Dean had taken two capfuls of the medicine, so I use about half a capful, mushing it together with the raw meat and then setting it on the floor at Charlie's feet. He gobbles it up eagerly, licks the dish clean, and then looks up at me with pleading eyes.

"You little pig." I smile, tear him off one more chunk, and feed it to him by hand before wrapping it back up and returning it to the refrigerator. "Well, maybe we'll all get a little peace now."

I pat Charlie on the head and then head over to the couch and open my laptop. I want to get a look at this ring on the big screen. Within minutes, I'm zoomed in on the engagement ring, analyzing the cut and quality and comparing it to the ring Dean gave me when we got engaged. There's no way he picked this one out himself—Jesika must have told him exactly what she wanted. I can just see them picking out the ring together, his hands cupping her still-flat stomach where their bastard offspring grows.

Bile rises in my throat, and I suddenly feel like I'm going to be sick. Setting my laptop to the side, I jump off the couch and run to the bathroom. I lose this morning's coffee in the toilet, tears and vomit mixing and causing an overwhelming sense of desperation to swell in my body. Dean never wanted kids—he didn't have the dad gene, he often said. But now, here he is, knocking up his home-wrecking girlfriend and putting a ring on it.

I fold my arms and hover over the toilet as my stomach heaves until I'm exhausted and my cheeks itch with salty tear tracks. I suck in slow, ragged breaths and try to control my body's rejection of their news. My body aches. I want a glass of wine to calm down, followed by a nap, but I can't today. As if on cue, Charlie scratches at the bathroom door.

"Oh, bugger off, you little bastard," I mumble, wiping at my tears as he scratches again. I stand, body aching as I stretch out the kinks in the bathroom mirror. Charlie scratches at the door again, and I cringe, realizing I'm not even with it enough at the moment to dog-sit. I assess my tired eyes in the mirror, thinking a week away in the desert would be nice. Maybe I've neglected myself over the last year, too focused on my career to focus on my marriage. I wonder then if Dean would be so cruel as to kick me out of the condo, leaving me homeless and with another nightmare to handle. I can only take so much heartache. I'd never known him to be so cruel in the past, but then, he seems to be a different man right now.

Charlie scratches again at the door, and a small whimper follows before I hear him plop onto the floor next to the door.

I inhale deeply, straighten my back, and then swing the door wide open. "There's a good boy."

My eyes narrow on the dog as I instantly realize something is wrong. Usually, he would be sleepy by now, relaxed and napping on the couch peacefully, but this is different. He's unable to focus his eyes on me and foam is bubbling at his mouth. He doesn't even seem strong enough to stand, and the scratching at the door was probably him kicking and thrashing his legs as he lost strength in his limbs.

Charlie looks like he's overdosing.

"Oh shit."

Chapter Seven

"I'm so sorry, Margaret." I fiddle with the leash; the feeble canine it's attached to won't be yanking my shoulder out of its socket anytime soon.

"Oh, dear, don't worry. Accidents happen. That dog is always putting things in his mouth he's not supposed to." Margaret pats my shoulder. I'm the one who should be comforting her, but I have so much guilt for what I've done to this woman's dog, I can't bring myself to stay a moment longer.

"If you need me to call anyone..." I sniff. "I tried to induce vomiting as much as I could, but I'm not sure it was enough."

What I don't tell her is that I spent twenty minutes shoving my fingers down this dog's throat in an effort to get up every last bit of raw hamburger and Benadryl. I then spent five minutes washing my hands with dish soap, and still the scent of dog vomit wafts in my nostrils.

"Sure, dear. Sure." Margaret glances down at the small limp body wrapped in a white blanket at her feet. Two paws stick out the front of the lifeless bundle, and it suddenly feels like I'm going to be sick again. "What did you say he got into again?"

"I'm not sure." I shrug. "Maybe something on our walk, a

toxic weed, maybe? I don't think it was anything from my house."

She only nods, bends feebly, and strokes one of Charlie's paws. "My brother-in-law is a veterinarian, maybe I could ask him what he thinks happened." I see tears hovering in her eyes, and I realize I've just possibly snatched away her most loyal companion. Charlie isn't dead...not yet anyway. I don't have much faith that he'll make it through the day with the lethargic way he's acting. The poor pup can hardly walk and it's all my fault, and watching her worry is making the sinking feeling in my chest worse.

"If there's anything you need, I'm always here." I hum, backing out of her front door. She doesn't say anything. "And if you need to take him to the vet, just send me the bill."

As soon as I'm out of her condo and the door is closed, I breathe a sigh of relief. My nerves are ravaged. The guilt of overdosing the woman's poor dog is more than I can take today. I head back to my condo next door and beeline for the wine rack as soon as I'm inside. I feel like I'm losing my grip on reality, the days stretching slowly in my wine-infused haze. Dean would have known what to do. He knew I liked to slip Charlie a Benadryl now and again to get some peace. He probably would have rolled his eyes at me and then called poison control or performed CPR or started some other life-saving action. That's Dean, always the hero. Except now. Now, he's someone else's hero. And he's going to be someone's dad. The thought makes my heart beat fast.

I pour Cabernet and swirl it in the glass, allowing it to breathe and the aroma to fill my nostrils. My nerves relax instantly. Pulling out the barstool, I take a seat at the kitchen island and take my first sip. I enjoy the way the wine heats my stomach. And then I remember the plan I had earlier.

It's dark, I know that, but I have to use every opportunity if

I'm going to make enough money to live off without Dean's income.

I pull out my phone, open Instagram, and hit the icon to create a new post.

I locate the photo of Charlie's fuzzy little paws sticking out of the blanket and add a little filter to make the shadows pop. I hit next on the screen once I'm happy with the adjustments and then hover over the box to write a caption. I imagine the outpouring of love and sympathy this photo will elicit. I have to strike just the right balance of sadness and resilience. First, I lose my husband to cancer and now my precious pooch—it's almost too much for a woman to bear.

Is it possible to die of a broken heart? I type swiftly. **My precious boy is gone but never forgotten —thank you for being such a good friend during the hardest moments of my life. My love picked you out from the litter when you were just a few weeks old. I know now you're running alongside him in heaven. RIP, Charlie.**

I pause a moment, rereading the caption, and then hit submit. My stomach flips as I think of all the attention this photo will generate. The dog may not be dead yet, but I'll find a way to make it work in my favor. If Dean knew I'd taken a photo of the nearly dead neighbor dog to boost my social media following, he'd call me a psychopath, but he's always been so quick to judge. Besides, maybe I wouldn't need to do it if he hadn't left me to fend for myself. In fact, it's basically Dean's fault that Charlie overdosed. If I hadn't been so stressed and on edge from their happy news, I wouldn't have slipped up and given Charlie too much Benadryl.

The poor pooch would still be running laps around me if not for my asshole ex and his new bubbly, bimbo girlfriend.

Chapter Eight

"So how was your weekend, Shae?" Kelly Fraser, LLP, has a voice that's made for psychotherapy. The octave low, the tone soothing as she strings out the constants in her words with slow precision. I wonder if she was born with the ability to speak like this or if it comes with the doctorate. She graduated from Northwestern the year I turned fifteen. I know because I've been staring at the degree mounted on the wall above her head once a week since then.

"Shae?" She interrupts my thoughts.

I press a hand to my forehead and feign exhaustion. "My weekend wasn't great. My neighbor's dog passed away unexpectedly. I used to take him for walks a few times a week to help her out, but I think those walks helped me out too." I even conjure a tear for full effect.

"Oh no. What happened?" Her concerned eyes warm as her body exudes pity.

"We're not sure. It looked like he had a seizure or something. I guess maybe he got into something he shouldn't have."

"Ah, poor doggy." She scratches something on her notepad

and then looks up at me. "So, not a great weekend. What about Dean? Have you heard from him at all?"

"Not really. I feel like a little kid in time-out. We hadn't even been fighting much lately. The way he just announced that he was leaving and then walked out... There's a better way to break the news than that, isn't there?" I swipe a tissue from the table and dab my eyes. "Overall, everything was fine. The weekend was fine. I'm just adapting to living alone and being with my own thoughts all the time and trying to stick to my old routines."

"Maybe call a friend for a coffee date or a hike in the mountains?"

"Maybe." I appreciate that she's trying to make me feel better, but it's not working. Making friends as an adult is hard. Most people have their established friend groups by this age, and since I work from home, I rarely get an opportunity to meet new people. "I had the worst nightmare last night. I dreamed a wildfire was coming down the canyon and everyone else was evacuated in time, but the lock on my door was stuck. I kept trying to get out, tried breaking a window, firefighters were trying to knock down the door, but nothing was working. I literally watched the fire come up my path and engulf the firefighters who were trying to save me. I watched them get burned alive, watched my condo go up in flames and take everything from me...and then right before it consumed me, I woke up."

"Oh." She frowns. "That sounds traumatic. Do you think it's a way for your mind to work out the recent trauma you've suffered?"

I only shrug, wondering what it is she's writing in that little lined notebook of hers. "What are you writing down?"

"Oh." She squints as she forms her reply. "Just that you've been having nightmares."

"I haven't been having nightmares. It's just this one."

"Were you thinking about anything stressful before you fell asleep?"

"No. Well, what isn't stressful these days?" I half laugh then slide my finger across the screen of my phone to wake it up. I frown, expecting at least a few notifications. "I think Dean is stalking me on social media."

"What makes you say that?" She's scribbling again. I want to snatch that little notebook from her and throw it out the window. Instead, I sit calmly, thumb swiping up on my screen absent-mindedly.

"I'm getting these comments on my posts from a guy I don't know. It looks like a burner account, and I know Dean would do that."

"Harass you online with a fake account?"

"Yeah. I should have blocked him the moment he walked out the door, but then I posted this picture with an empty wine bottle and I was too late..." I shake my head. So many regrets.

"What kind of things are they commenting?"

I pause, wondering if I should tell her the full truth. I decide on a watered-down version. "I found out on social media this weekend that Jesika is pregnant."

"Who is Jesika?"

Shit. I didn't mean to use her real name. "His new girlfriend. And they're engaged. He never wanted kids when we were together," I say sadly. My stomach lurches uncomfortably at just the memory of the engagement announcement she posted. "So I know they're motivated to get the divorce moving along. I don't even have the heart to read the divorce papers, but I did skim the page that divided our assets. Bastard didn't list all the investments I know he's got, and he's offering a very small stipend per month in lieu of alimony." My blood begins to boil as I think back on it. "So Saturday, I log in to my social media account and come across a few comments from a guy who isn't even following me—obviously, he knows what's going on. One comment just said 'LIAR' in shouty caps. Another comment said 'do the right thing or else.' I dread logging in to social media now." That last part isn't exactly true, but it sounds good. "I've had trolls before, it happens, but this just feels personal."

"Hmm." She scribbles some more shit in her notebook and avoids my gaze. "What do you think they meant by or else?"

I shrug, annoyed that she's being so calm. "Dean is crazy. When he gets angry, he just fixates on destroying whatever is in front of him. He was supposed to be working on that in therapy, but who knows if he's even still going now that he's got Jesika." I can't help the disdain that leaks into my tone when I say her name.

"This situation has been very difficult. A few months ago, weren't you discussing how toxic things had gotten between the two of you? Fighting more and concerned that he was spending more time at work and not with you? Is there some relief that you finally know what's been going on, why he's been so distant?"

"Relief?" I'm shocked. "You think I should be relieved?"

"I don't think you should feel anything but how you're feeling." She waits a beat and then continues. "Dean was also frustrated with the social media aspect of your business, wasn't he?" I nod, wondering where this is leading. "Maybe it's time to shut down the account for a while."

"You think I should kill my online persona?" I frown.

"Kill the brand, at least. Have you thought about what that would look like?"

"Yeah, it would look like me living in a tent on Skid Row."

She chuckles and shakes her head. "You're so funny, you could be a comedian. So maybe next week, we can work on some coping mechanisms for when you're feeling emotionally overcome. I think I have some handouts that might shift your perspective on this."

"Hm." I swipe at my phone again as the therapist closes her notebook and tucks it between her thigh and the chair arm. She stands, catching my eye and smiling easily. "Is our session over already?"

Kelly nods. "It is, but you know you're welcome to reach out via email or text anytime if you're struggling."

I nod, thinking how I would never do that. In fact, I'm sure this is something therapists just say so you feel supported. The reality of clients reaching out after hours must be a nightmare. I'm thankful for her gesture just the same, though. "You seem distracted today, Doc."

My therapist catches my gaze, eyes lingering for a long moment as if she's considering revealing more about herself. "You're very perceptive."

I smile, only watching her watch me. I've been seeing this woman for almost two decades, and I hardly know if I'd recognize her on the street. I'm so used to seeing her only in the context of this room, my pain and frustration the sole topic of all of our conversations. I wonder what she thinks of me, really. I imagine snatching her little notebook and running off with it just to find out.

"My sister is moving this weekend. She's on a plane now, and I have to be at the airport in an hour to pick her up. She's been working overseas for the last two years, teaching at an English school in Shanghai and having all of these incredible adventures. I'm a little nervous to see her, I suppose. She's staying with me until she can find a place to rent, but I swear she was born a rolling stone. She'll probably have a flight booked by the end of the week to some new exotic locale. We're so different...our likes and dislikes are worlds apart, but she's the only family I have left, so I try to embrace all the differences that make us *us*."

Kelly's eyes track up and down my form before she smiles and continues, "You look like her, actually. Same hair color and bone structure, even the same big, round eyes. She's beautiful and statuesque, and in truth, I've always felt a little self-conscious around her." Kelly places a hand on her thick waist. "I've been struggling to lose the same fifty pounds for a decade, and being thin and active just seems to come naturally to her."

I nod, smile sweetly, and then reply, "Well, I'm sure you'll have a great time with your sister—what did you say her name was again?"

"Oh, I didn't. But it's Katie. Katie and Kelly. So original, right?"

"Sounds like twins."

"We don't look like twins. In fact, you could probably pass for her sister more than me. People usually mistake us for mother and daughter when we go out."

I nod, suddenly filled with curiosity about Kelly Fraser, LLP's personal life. "Well, have a great rest of your week, Doc."

I can't get out of the office fast enough. I bet I could find my therapist on social media and then search her list of followers to find her beautiful and statuesque sister Katie. I could follow both of them under Mia's account, and neither of them would be the wiser. I could be a fly on the wall of their lives and not have to worry about the weird patient-doctor confidentiality thing that I signed in my new client paperwork.

By the time I hit the elevator, I'm pulling up Instagram on my phone. Before I can get to the search bar, though, the app loads and takes me directly to my newsfeed, where I find Jesika's latest post.

Dammit. Fucking shit.

It's them. Together. The new, happily engaged couple side

by side. It's the first time she's shared Dean's face—and it's not even his full face, but it's enough of his smile and beard lingering over her shoulder at some hipster eatery that I can confirm it's my husband. My no-good, piece-of-shit spouse is wining and dining his new favorite toy, and I'm left to cry out my feelings on a therapist's couch. Anger swirls in my stomach as I zoom in on the photo, looking for any details to identify their location. I notice then that she tagged her nonalcoholic—according to her caption—cocktail with the restaurant they're at: Hominy. I know that place—a new and trendy West Hollywood joint creating modern dishes with a homestyle twist. She posted this in the last hour. Is it possible they're still there? What would I do if I ran into them out in public? I suddenly find myself obsessed with the idea.

It's then I realize that her post contains multiple photos. I swipe to the left on the first photo and then almost lose my lunch all over my sneakers.

It's them. Naked. In bed. *Together.*

I can only see part of his face again, but I notice the freckles across his bare shoulder. The way she's tucked into his arm, giant toothy grin on her face and that glittery, ostentatious engagement ring she's wearing on her ring finger.

I hate them.

I hate them so much I can taste it rising in my throat like bile.

Dean has no idea what he did that day he chose to walk out on me. Has no idea the string of events he unleashed when he announced he wanted a divorce. And now, all I can think about is how my husband deserves to suffer for the pain his new life is inflicting on me.

Chapter Nine

New man. New baby. New city!

I cringe when Jesika's latest Instagram pops up.

"New city?" I hum, mind instantly on fire with the possibilities. The photo shows Jesika, smiling ear to ear among stacks of moving boxes with floor-to-ceiling windows and a skyline view behind her.

Chicago.

I know it's Chicago because that's where Jesika is from. I vaguely remember a Chicago address listed on the model release forms we signed over a year ago. How in the world did she get Dean to move across the country? I save the photo to my phone, mostly so I can study that skyline and find out exactly where they're living. The next thing I do, without even a second thought, is book a flight to Chicago. I've never been there, and I was always begging Dean to travel with me, but he was always too busy with work. Bitterness blooms within me before I take a few deep breaths and hit submit on the payment for my flight and then begin my search for a hotel.

I guess I'm leaving in the morning. I'm not sure what I'll do once I arrive, but I'll figure it out on the fly. I just have the sense that I need to see them together once to confirm it's real. To confirm that the man I married really is a piece of shit. Then I can move on. I'll sign the divorce papers and give the cheating asshole what he wants. But giving him what he deserves sounds way more fun.

For the next hour, I pack some essentials for the trip and let my mind roll around ideas of revenge. I take a coffee break and do an internet search: *how to get revenge on your ex*. But the ideas are mostly silly and only make me laugh. I even think to send a text message to my therapist that I'll be out of town a few days and we'll have to skip our next session. She doesn't answer me, and I wonder if her sister is still in town and how it's going. It's only been a few days since I last left her office. I haven't hardly had time to think about healthy coping mechanisms, and then it hits me. Dean and Jesika in Chicago. I can't just sit back and do nothing, right? Is he even allowed to leave the state of California when there are pending legal proceedings in play? I haven't signed the divorce papers yet, and now, maybe I won't.

Maybe the way to punish this man for all the pain he's caused is to deny him what he now wants—a new family.

This thought carries me through all of my four-hour flight the following morning, and I hit the ground at O'Hare with a vague plan. I'm determined to find a way to split them up...so far my best idea is to get hired as Jesika's assistant or house-cleaner. If I can wiggle myself into Jesika's life and make friends with her, maybe I can drive a wedge between them. In fact, I won't stop until I do.

I slip into the idling taxicab and point the driver to a luxury hotel and spa on the east side of the city. I'm positive they're staying nearby because I spent all night scrolling through photos of hotels and comparing the view of the city with Jesika's *new man, new baby, new city* post. I'm pretty sure I can see a slice of

Lake Michigan in the distance and what looks like some of
Millennium Park too. The neighborhood looks fancy, and if I'm
going to have a chance at running into Jesika, I'm going to have
to camp out nearby.

The cab driver drops me off in front of the Foundry Hotel,
and even though it's early afternoon, the February wind still
carries a chill. As I step out of the cab, I feel a sense of relief. Is
this what my therapist wanted for me? Setting goals and chasing
my dreams feels good. On some level, I'm aware that maybe this
isn't the healthy coping mechanism she had in mind, but right
now, the feeling is giving me life when nothing else has, so I'm
embracing it.

With a sense of eagerness, I stroll into the lobby of the
Foundry with newfound confidence. And Dean's Amex card in
my pocket. I found the matte black credit card among a stack of
files he must have forgotten in the file cabinet. I'm surprised he
hasn't asked for it, but then, why would he, when he can just as
easily call the company and have the card shut off and a new
one mailed to him. Maybe it slipped his mind, or maybe he
didn't have a current mailing address, considering the chaos of
the move to Chicago. I considered spending all of the available
credit limit on it, but for the first time in my adult life, I can
support myself, and so I booked the penthouse for the next two
weeks at the Foundry using my own cash from the GoFundMe
and Patreon page that I deposited into my account.

Walking up to the check-in desk, I feel like I'm on top of the
world. And once I offer my name, Mia Starr, the employee's
face lights up.

"We're so pleased to be your home away from home, Ms.
Starr. I hope the trip wasn't too arduous for you." The woman
smiles, her eyes glancing down to the large canary diamond on
my finger and then back up to my eyes. "Ms. Starr has arrived,"
she says as the concierge pauses at her shoulder.

"Welcome." The elderly gentleman nods and then bends to retrieve something below the desk. They must have a wine fridge, because he's uncorking a bottle of champagne and then pouring me a glass with a grin.

"Why thank you!" I take the bubbling glass from him and sip. "It's lovely."

"Only the best for our most cherished guests." I feel utterly catered to, and it's all the assurance I need for having spent nearly $14,000 for the next two weeks. The card I'm using is connected to an account Dean and I share, so he could log in and see what I've been up to, but something tells me he's got his head too far up Jesika's ass to even notice what I'm doing. A flashback of one of the troll comments from a stranger on my Instagram comes back to me. Maybe he's not that busy, or maybe there's a chance it wasn't even him. I'm still not sure, and every time I log in to my account, a niggling sense of dread takes root in my stomach.

"Can I show you to your suite, Ms. Starr?" A bellboy dressed in all red is at my side with a friendly smile.

"Sure. Just give me a moment to snap a quick photo of this gorgeous lobby."

"Would you like me to be your photographer?" The bellboy is already reaching for my phone.

"Oh no. No thanks." I grip my phone tightly. "I don't like to take photos of myself."

He nods politely and pretends not to watch as I snap a quick shot of my champagne in one hand and the chandelier dripping with crystals that hangs in the center of the lobby in the background. An elegant fountain bubbles beneath it, a statue of two cherubs midflight, reaching out as if they're trying to touch the crystals above their curly heads. It radiates the illusion of wealth and elegance. Now I'll just need to come up with a clever caption that doesn't reveal where exactly I am. If Dean really is watching my account, I can't have him aware that I'm now in the same city he is. Heck, he probably wanted a break from LA —a break from me—and now, here I am.

Setting goals and chasing dreams, just like Mia Starr would do.

Chapter Ten

B **lessed**

\# Smiling to myself, I hit submit on a series of candid shots. I know I shouldn't feel blessed, and the truth is, I don't. I've just lost my husband and my dog. I feel like shit, but I'm sick of all the wallowing that's been happening on my Instagram feed lately, so I'm testing the waters with a gratitude post. My life is great, and I'm determined to put one foot in front of the other and cultivate the life I want. It's what Mia would do. She wouldn't lose herself in the pain and heartache. She would bounce back with her head held high. It's been weird, splitting myself between two different personalities, so I've decided not to do it anymore.

I've decided to embrace Mia's presence in my life. I always have; it's one of the things Dean used to complain about—that I was too wrapped up in Mia to live my life. But what life do I have to live? Mia's persona has given me so much. Why would I dial back Mia to find Shae again? Shae is boring and sad, the opposite of Mia's wild and beautiful existence.

The notifications on my latest post of the champagne in the lobby and the skyline from my suite are already starting to ping my phone. I ignore them, pour more of the bubbly into my glass and then swipe to the camera lens on my phone. I hold it up to the window, trying to focus my eyes on the golden-lit windows of the buildings in my direct line of sight. I've done my best to triangulate the location of Dean and Jesika's new place based on the single photo she posted. I know they're north of Millennium Park and maybe a little to the west—as far as I can tell, they're right here somewhere. I've even tried to compare details of the brickwork in her photo to the buildings in this area. Most in this area—known as the Loop by locals—is a mix of residential brownstones and historic buildings and warehouses that have been remodeled into apartments.

I know I shouldn't fixate like this. Mia Starr would definitely be too busy to fixate on her ex, but Mia would also have friends in every city around the world. Awareness crushes my enthusiasm when I realize if I hadn't started this ruse with Jesika, the model representing Mia Starr online, I could both reach out to my followers and have a get-together here tonight in Chicago. And maybe, just maybe, my husband wouldn't have left me for a slightly younger and hotter me.

Revenge coils in my stomach like a snake about to strike before I push that thought out of my head and refocus on what's in front of me.

Dean and Jesika's new life is somewhere out there, within a few blocks of me if I had to bet. I vow then that I will stop at nothing to track them down. I just need a glimpse. I need to see what Dean thinks he's been missing. I need to know why walking away from an entire life is worth it.

My gaze scans the tiny lit windows as I watch for a familiar face among strangers. Would I recognize Jesika in person? I only know her from her various posed and candid photos that we purchased for the brand, first existing photos and then from the commissioned photo shoot later. I imagine what Dean must have thought when he first met her in real life—did she remind him of me? How could she not? He picked her out because he said we had the same high cheekbones and long white-gold hair. It hurts that he's effectively replaced me, but I won't let it hurt for long. I'll bring his new fiancée down a few pegs—I'm still his wife after all. At least on paper.

And then I choke on my next breath when a familiar sheet of shiny blond hair catches my eye. A woman is standing with her back to the window, her only striking feature the wave of platinum that falls down her back. Even from this angle, it's obvious she's gorgeous. I try to zoom in on my camera, but the view only gets grainier.

It's her. I'm positive of it.

My suspicion is confirmed when my good-for-nothing, cheating ex-husband comes into view and wraps his arms around her small waist. He dips his head, snuggles into her neck, and then she wraps her arms around his body and melts into him. I remember that feeling, the sense of safety his warm embrace brings. A shiver runs through me now as I struggle to remember the last time I felt that feeling—his body against mine, murmuring that everything will be okay. It's been months. And then it hits me that one of my favorite things—Dean's hugs —have been absent from my life for far longer than I realized. How is it that I could let one of my favorite things fall away so easily? When did it happen? Was there a deciding event that pushed us apart? A fight or miscommunication or words misspoken? When did I move from the wife to the villain role in his life?

I watch, transfixed on the loving couple in the building across from me. Tears burn my eyelids as I realize I've followed them here, only to prolong my own heartache. I'm practically a masochist, torturing myself with their love.

And then the very worst happens.

Jesika turns to face the window, and with Dean's arms around her waist, I imagine she feels like she's on top of the world. I swallow the painful ball lodged in my throat and watch through tears as their bodies begin to move in a familiar rhythm.

They're making love, right in front of the window.

Right in front of me.

A fresh wave of revenge consumes me as I watch them, his hands on her waist holding her against him as her palms splay against the floor-to-ceiling windows. Dean is rough when he makes love, frenzied and aggressive and practically insatiable. I loved his hands in my hair. Sometimes a quick spanking on my ass would send a thrill of need through me. I wonder if she likes it like I did, the way he makes love to her. Or maybe he's different with her, maybe she brings out the tender side of his love.

Without thinking, I smack my hand against the cold window, and it hurts—my fingertips tingling with pain adding to the tears that are filling my eyes.

And then my heart stops.

Jesika's eyes look up, as if something has caught her attention. Or someone. It's as if she's looking right at me, her gaze focusing on mine while my husband fucks her. I drop my phone and back away from the window, suddenly feeling like I've been caught. A sense of shame bubbles up in my veins. If I'm going to really do this, I'll need to be much more careful. If Dean catches me, he'll without a doubt blow up my life and rework the divorce agreement to ensure I get absolutely nothing.

I groan, stripping out of the hotel bathrobe and taking my bottle of champagne to the bathroom. Within minutes, I'm slipping into a relaxing bubble bath, my mind swirling with visions of Dean fucking my Mia.

I hate him. I hate him so much I could kill him.

Chapter Eleven

Morning sunshine melts the condensation off the Michigan Avenue sign as I pass. I walk by a Starbucks on the corner of Lake, and the line at this time of morning nearly wraps the block. I can't imagine being so addicted to caffeine that I'd wait in line for thirty minutes every day. I overhear a conversation between two women as I pass. One is talking about dropping their daughter off at preschool before nearly missing her hot yoga class.

A frown slips past my lips as the thought crosses my mind that that's how normal people connect. Over coffee and small talk and the day's commiserations. I envy them; I do. The ease with which they play off each other, the language between them is easy and flows. I've never had that kind of friendship. I wonder briefly why that is and think that might be something to bring up in my next therapy session. I'm kind of missing Kelly Fraser, LLP. I wonder how the weekend with her sister went. I don't know why I'm intrigued by them. Having a sister must be blessing and a curse. On the one hand, you have a built-in buddy—when you're not dancing around emotional land mines, that is. Something about women in relationships makes me feel on edge, like I don't quite belong.

My stomach chooses that moment to rumble a reminder that I haven't eaten yet today. I did not get up for a morning hot yoga class, even though I know the fitness center in the Foundry offers one. Instead, I slept in and willed the flashbacks of Jesika and Dean's window-bang session from the night before out of my mind. I figured some cool morning air would do me good and help me get the lay of the neighborhood.

As if on cue, a woman wearing stylish black Chelsea boots exits a limestone entryway with a chic black awning. A wave of metallic blond hair falls down her back, and a ripple of aware-ness shoots through me.

It's her. I know it is.

I've found them. This must be their building. It seems farther away from the street than it did last night, watching them through the window.

Had they seen me watching?

Is there a chance she could recognize me?

Fear dampens my resolve, and I stumble a few steps, eyes watching as she speed walks down the sidewalk like she's made this hike a hundred times. Maybe a thousand. She reaches the next street and continues to walk like she's late for an appoint-ment. I nearly lose her in the small crowd as we approach the start of Millennium Park on the east side of the street. Tourists jostle and move around us, but I stick with my target, her striking blond hair standing out in a crowd. I'm struggling to keep up with her, and I'm only wearing some old fur-and-leather-trimmed boots. She's in low-heeled boots that would be pinching my feet in pain already. How does she make pain look so elegant? It must be a talent she was born with, I swallow down my growing sense of jealousy as the crowd thins and it's mostly just her and me again.

By the time we reach Monroe Avenue and the end of the park, I'm struggling to catch my breath. Clearly, I'm out of shape, compared to this woman. No wonder she caught Dean's eye. He's banging the new-and-improved version of me. Something in me wants to tell her, make her see how he's using her somehow. Maybe I could have something delivered to their apartment, an envelope with a USB thumb drive with a video of Dean and me being intimate. It's then I realize that we never were kinky enough to turn on the camera. Dean likes rough sex, but it was often over fast. We never lingered long or spent time trying new things. I wish now we had. Although I would no doubt torture myself watching the videos on repeat.

I bet Jesika and Dean try new and kinky things all the time.

A tear catches me by surprise, and I wipe at it, feeling overwhelmed enough with emotion that I want to stop Jesika—explain everything woman-to-woman. Maybe she would understand; maybe she would admit that she didn't even realize he was married. What an asshole! We could commiserate together over our morning coffee and be best friends. And then suddenly, as if she's heard me, Jesika turns and glances behind her once and then ducks into a coffee shop with a red-checkered awning.

Without thinking, I dart in after her.

I don't know what I'm going to say, but I have to say something to the woman who stole my husband.

Chapter Twelve

"A double chai oat milk latte, please." The young woman standing in front of me at the Roastery has a lilt in her tone that's jarring. Saccharine positivity bleeds from her words. I don't think I've ever been as eager to order an overpriced latte as she sounds right now.

I force a smile on my face as I wait for her to pay. She's digging through her leather shoulder bag, smile finally turning to a frown as she realizes she's forgotten something.

"I must have left my wallet at home." The saccharine positivity is traded for dejected worry. She turns, catches my eyes once, and mouths a soft apology.

I inwardly cringe and outwardly smile.

"Let me pay." I move around her form and pass the barista my credit card. The line is long behind us, and I have little patience for forgetfulness. I've never forgotten my wallet anywhere, but I don't mind paying it forward to a stranger.

Anyway, we're not strangers. She just doesn't know my face yet.

"Are you sure? I feel like such an idiot."

"Don't." *Do,* I think.

I realized long ago that the happiness of life is made up of the smallest, soon-forgotten moments of kindness. A smile exchanged with a stranger, a heartfelt compliment, or, in this case, an overpriced oat milk latte. It's not that I'm looking for a friend or that I'm even being sincere in my offering, but I find it easier to get what I want out of life if I'm willing to put some effort into the tiniest of pleasantries.

Jesika smiles sweetly, mouthing a thank-you and then moving away from the counter to wait for her latte. I order my almond milk cappuccino, pay for both of us, and then move down the counter to wait with her. I fumble with my wallet, trying to slip my credit card back in its correct slot, when, instead, it flings from my hand and skitters across the counter. My shiny black Amex with my real name, Shae Halston, lands directly in front of her.

I make an audible *oof* noise and reach for it, but she beats me to it, picking it up and holding it in the light that's streaming through the window. "Cool card. It's like a hologram. My fiancé has a credit card like this." She passes it back to me with a friendly wink. "I'm Jesika."

I know, I think.

"Maya." The lie comes quickly as I shove my card back in the slot of my wallet.

"Nice to meet you. I've been coming here to work a little every morning. It's the nearest coffee shop to our new apartment. I've never seen you, though."

I only nod, not expecting how open she is. No wonder Dean likes her. Where I am reticent, she is an open book.

"You're new to the city?" I speak like I've been living in Chicago all my life. In reality, I'm just as new as they are.

"Yes. We moved about a month ago. My boyfriend has been dealing with some stuff back home, so it seemed like the right time for a move. A fresh start and all that."

"Dealing with stuff?" I ask.

She nods, eyes fluttering as she brushes a stray lock of platinum out of her eyes. "His crazy ex can't let go."

I am the *stuff* he's been dealing with. I had a hunch, and now Jesika has confirmed it.

"I just signed the lease on my new apartment here so it seemed like the perfect time to move in together." She smiles sweetly, and venom thickens in my veins.

"Are you married?" she asks politely.

"No—never." I nearly choke on the lie. "My ex was a hot mess, I'm still recovering."

She laughs. "Oh my God, aren't they all? Can't live with them but can you imagine a world without them? It's not a world I'd want to live in." She chuckles.

Our drinks come at the same time, and I lift mine to my lips to cover the frown on my face. I hate her already. Maybe I always have, but now the hate is hardening like cement in my bloodstream.

"Join me?" Jesika gestures to a nearby table. "I don't know a single soul in this city anymore. All my friends had babies and moved to the 'burbs. It would be nice to have a friend downtown to sip expensive lattes with."

She's so nice.

I'm trying to hold on to my hate, but she's getting to me. Getting under my skin with her genuine smile, and I can't have that. I've got a plan, and becoming friends with Jesika Layman isn't on my to-do list.

"I have a meeting with an advertiser in an hour, but sure," I lie.

We sit at the table, settling in like old friends, before she asks, "An advertiser? What do you do?"

"It's not as important as it sounds. I..." I didn't plan for this little *tête-à-tête*, so I struggle to couch my answer in dishonesty.

"I have a blog. A company wants to send me some products to try, that's all. It's nothing fancy."

"Oh! You're an influencer?" Her eyes brighten.

"I guess they call it that." I sip. The hot liquid burns my throat. It grounds me, snaps me out of my haze. I'm playing with fire here; even I know that. If Jesika finds out who I really am, she'll run right back to Dean, and he'll lose it. *Again.* I can't afford a single misstep.

"What kind of products do you advertise?"

I'm struggling to lie on the fly again. If I reveal too much, she'll go home and tell Dean about her new influencer friend, and he'll know immediately that it's me. "Fashion...for dogs."

"Oh, you have a dog? I've always wanted a dog, but Dean, my fiancé, is allergic."

And there it is. She's used his name for the first time, and I hope she doesn't catch the visceral reaction that crosses my face when she says it.

"That's too bad. I don't know where I would be without my fur baby. My husband cheated on me, just up and left with his new girlfriend a few months ago. Mitzi has gotten me through the cold, lonely nights. I know it's cliché, but I don't have a lot of friends either, and the few I did have hated my husband—they could see through him better than I could, I guess. Always listen to your friends, especially if they don't like your spouse. There's a reason for it, that's the lesson I've learned."

"I'm sorry." A look of pity muddies her otherwise perfect features.

She's not as pretty as the photos, I think finally. There's a reason we picked her, but if we'd met her in person, I don't think I would have. She's not Mia Starr. Not like I made her out to be in my mind anyway.

"So, are you from Chicago?" She sips and purrs.

I shake my head, uncomfortable with this question. "Vegas —I was living in Vegas for a while before I came here."

"Oh, fun city. I haven't been there in a few years. It must be a trip to actually live there."

"Yeah, it sure is. Well, I need to do some research on the company I'm meeting with. I should get going." Seeing my Mia sitting across from me is starting to make my skin crawl. An odd mix of disappointment and rage floods my system the longer we sit across from each other.

"Oh." She looks genuinely disappointed. "Maybe we could exchange phone numbers and meet up for a drink sometime?"

"Oh, I don't know…" I didn't expect the scent of desperation that's wafting off her. Don't girls like this one collect friends wherever they go? That's the impression I get scrolling my newsfeed anyway. "I'm sure I'll see you here again. I come about the same time every morning."

"Okay." She seems sad. Does Jesika really want to be friends with me? Girls like her usually find one another—fabulous girls flock together, buzzing around the hot spots in any given city like flies on shit.

Resentment bubbles as I stand from my chair.

"Have a great day." Peppy positivity laces my words as she smiles up at me.

"Thanks for the latte, Maya. It's so good to know there are still nice people out there. The next round is on me." She holds her hot drink up in a gesture of cheers.

I only nod, already turning to escape her bright smile.

I step into the crisp morning air and inhale. I was surprised when I found out Jesika and Dean were moving to Chicago, so dreary and industrial compared to our sunshine-soaked hamlet on the California coast, but the city energy suits me, I'm finding. It's just the change of scenery I need. I turn down Michigan Avenue, long strides carrying me away from Jesika and closer to my new life. It feels good to no longer pretend to be Maya, but then, maybe I *could* be Maya, best friend to Jesika Layman. Maybe it's time I bury Shae Halston and become the kind of girl that has fabulous friends and cocktail dates filling her schedule.

And then I remember the plan. A wry smile turns my lips.

Jesika and Maya will never be friends.

Shae is going to kill her first.

Chapter Thirteen

I can't stop thinking about her.

It's not surprising because I've been trying to adapt myself to her routine the last few days. I even picked up some cheap binoculars just in case Dean and Jesika made a special repeat performance at their picture window.

They haven't yet. But I've been checking fastidiously. I know they'll be back; I just need to be patient. And now that I know Jesika stops by the Roastery across from Millennium Park every morning around nine a.m., it's much easier for me to coincidently run into her. I haven't talked to her again. I've been trying to keep my distance as she picks up her morning coffee, then walks the perimeter of the park for a while before veering off Michigan Avenue to pop into a yoga studio. After yoga, she either grabs a smoothie and walks back to their apartment building, or sometimes she walks to a building in the Financial District that overlooks the river. I imagine she's taking meetings with her agent or business manager, maybe much like the one she would have taken over a year ago when Dean and I decided to hire her for the Mia Starr job.

I regret not flying to Chicago and meeting with her in

person back then. It feels like, somehow, things would have been different. If she'd met me—seen my face—would she still have been willing to fuck my husband? She doesn't seem like the cold and ruthless home-wrecker type, but then, neither do I, and I most certainly have been one in the past.

I pause, taking in the famous glossy, metallic Millennium Park Bean. Distorted images of my face reflect back at me like I'm in an alternate-reality fun house, my nose larger than life at one angle, eyes large and round at another. I'm looking at a version of myself that's been fractured into a dozen warped pieces. It's familiar, but not quite right at the same time and leaves me feeling exposed in a way I didn't expect.

Sipping my hot oat milk latte, I turn and walk in the direction of Lake Michigan as I muse on what it would be like to have Jesika's life. I've already switched to her morning drink of choice. The chill of the wind coming off the lake bites at my cheeks as I get closer to the lakeshore. Traffic rushes down Lakeshore Drive, and I'm so caught up in my head musing about Jesika's life that I nearly step into oncoming traffic. A Subaru holds down the horn, and the noise is enough to shake me from my thoughts. As the pedestrian crossing light indicates it's my time to cross, a gust of wind steals my breath and causes me to falter a step. My coffee jostles just enough that a splash of the hot liquid scalds the skin of my hand. I cuss, tears coming to my eyes as I think how much I hate the Windy City.

Nothing about it appeals to me, from the constant rush of traffic to the icy wind and the cold personalities to match. I conjure the warmth of the LA sunshine on my skin as I finally reach the Lake Michigan coastline. Gray skies bleed into the mist that hovers over the water. The last breath of winter floats in the form of chunks of ice on the frigid waves. The water is deep and dark, and an ominous feeling clings to the shore and my shoulders like a storm cloud. Determined to shake the chill, I walk on quick steps back across the park. Instead of heading the way I came, I head south toward Grant Park and Buckingham Fountain. The rich green patina of the marble-and-bronze fountain matches my mood. I've been practically green with envy from the moment I found out about Jesika, and now here I am, following her around the Windy City like it's my job.

A small family on electric scooters zips by me, and I have to sidestep to avoid getting clipped by what looks like a ten-year-old. I resist yelling at the kid and instead take a seat on the nearest bench. Seated along the edge of Millennium Park has proven to be a relaxing activity. I feel like I'm a part of the morning hustle, like I have places to go and people to see. Just like Jesika. And then, speak of the devil, she appears across the street. While I was nearly in a hit-and-run accident with a kid on a scooter, she must have walked into the Roastery. Now, she's walking out and crossing at the nearest crosswalk, just like she always does. I can see the steam from her coffee curling in tendrils around her head, sunlight hitting her like a halo. The wind whips up her shiny golden hair, and I think how utterly perfect she is. Really, no wonder Dean is in love with her. I think I am too, but not in the same way. I'm fixated, for sure. I can't let it bother me. Love is a delusion anyway, at least in my experience.

Besides, I don't want to own this woman—I want to *be* this woman. I already am, as far as the internet is concerned.

At that moment, I realize I should be taking full advantage of this situation, and I pull out my phone. I line up the angle just right so it looks like a well-posed but still candid photo. I snap away as she crosses the street, sips her coffee, then stops at a nearby bench and watches the fountain for a while. I'm transfixed by her, coveting the life she is living that was once mine. She has no idea what she's taken from me, but then, I think she deserves whatever is coming to her. Certainly, she knows Dean is the man who hired her for the social media photo shoots over a year ago. Neither of our names is on the contract, but the name of our corporation is, and a quick internet search of that would reveal both of our real names.

Jesika is scrolling on her phone now, and then she pauses to type out a quick message to someone before going back to her scrolling again. I snap another few photos and imagine the caption I'll use when I upload them to my Instagram profile. I tuck my phone away and sip my coffee as I consider the lucky position I've found myself in. If I stay at a distance from Jesika but close enough to take candid photos every now and again, I can basically get photos and content for free for my page. I'll never have to buy Jesika's photos again.

Jesika takes that moment to glance my way, and I wonder if she's recognized me.

I wave halfheartedly and then think better of it and stand, waltzing toward her with a smile on my face.

She sees me now, recognition lifting her smile before she jumps up from her spot on the bench and walks to me quickly. "It's so good to see you again!"

"Hi!" I force a smile.

She wraps me in a warm hug and then gestures for me to sit with her on the bench. She's so easy to be friends with, so welcoming. It takes me by surprise. I don't think I've ever inter- acted with the world this way. Like every stranger is a friend.

"I think this is a sign we should be friends. Two meetings in one week!"

"Yeah." I don't know how to respond.

"Hey, are you available tonight? I have reservations at this super-cool new underground speakeasy. You need a passcode and everything to get in. I've heard the best things! My fiancé is too busy working, and the girlfriend I was supposed to go with got booked for a shoot in LA at the last minute."

"Oh no, I couldn't."

"Of course you can. Why can't you?" She laughs and bumps against my shoulder as she does. The contact is jarring, like a reminder of why I'm here.

"Well, I just don't usually—"

"Oh please. I make a habit of doing things I don't usually do. You should try it. There's an adventure just waiting for you!"

"An adventure, huh?" My smile lifts because her enthusiasm is infectious.

"An epic one. Let's meet up at my place first. It's just a few blocks up Michigan. We'll have a little aperitif, and you can meet my fiancé!" My blood runs cold with her words.

"Oh no, I don't think I can handle that much adventure. How about I meet you there? Do you know the address?"

"Okay! I'll text it to you! The reservation is for eight. Type your phone number in, and I'll link you." She holds out her phone, and I suddenly realize I should have snagged a burner phone for just this moment. It's a risk, giving Jesika my real phone number, but the likelihood that she shows Dean is slim to none, so I do as she instructed and quickly type in my number. A moment later, my phone buzzes with her incoming message.

"Oh, it looks great." The thumbnail that pops up is dark and moody, like an intimate cocktail bar and the perfect vibe for intimate conversations.

"Told you, you're gonna love it! The passcode this month is 5-2-5-7, they change it the first day of every month. I used to date one of the bartenders there—not great in bed, but worth it for my monthly text with the passcode for Brando's."

"That sounds so cool. I love places like this. You know me so well already."

"I'm super great with people. I think we're soul sisters, I have a feeling." She winks and then sips the last of her drink. "I have a business meeting in twenty minutes. It's only a few blocks away. Do you want to walk with me?"

"No, I have...some stuff to do today." I can't reveal more because, in truth, I *have* been walking with her the last few mornings. She just hasn't realized it.

"Okay, well, I'll see you tonight, then?" Her eyes are warm and hopeful as she regards me.

"I can't wait." I glance down her form and then add, "I love those boots."

"Oh, thanks. I've had them forever. They're vintage Versace." She smiles sweetly.

My eyes round. Of course they're vintage *something*. "They'd look so great on my blog."

Her eyes narrow, and I know instantly my mistake.

"I thought your blog was about dog fashions?" Her eyebrows scrunch together.

"Yeah, it is. It's both. You know how they say dogs often look like their owners?" She doesn't reply but gives me an odd look. "It's kinda like that."

"Oh." She nods. "Well, see ya later, then?"

I force a grin and wave, watching her walk away as I realize I just dodged my first bullet with Jesika, and I can't afford any more. I'll have to be careful with my words and even more careful with my thoughts. Jesika is as vain and superficial as I imagined she'd be, but she's not dumb.

And underestimating her could prove to be a costly mistake.

Chapter Fourteen

o you want to schedule a video call for your session this week?

I cringe when I realize I forgot to reschedule my appointment with Kelly Fraser, LLP. I'm not even sure how long I'll be in Chicago, and I know if I miss too many appointments, she'll start to push about why. I've told my therapist a lot about my life. I've opened up about my marriage, but I can't tell her this—that I've come to Chicago with revenge on my mind. Heck, I don't even know what that means, really, but I know I need to figure it out. I just keep thinking that all the closure I need is in seeing them together. If I see them, if I know they're really in love, then maybe somehow I'll be able to go back to California with my head held high. I'll grant Dean the divorce he wants, and then I can move on from this painful part of my life.

I have plans this evening, but maybe at the end of the week? I reply quickly, then put down my phone and take in my reflection in the vanity mirror. My hair is curled into soft waves, my eyeliner is winged and thick, and my cheekbones are contoured to a fine chisel. I look like I should be on a reality show about wealthy housewives. I don't feel like myself at all, but maybe that's the point.

Friday works for me. I add.

Great to hear you have plans! Reaching out and embracing community is so essential for healing. Looking forward to chatting on Friday—around 3, maybe? Kelly's text is immediate.

Perfect, is all I reply before tossing my phone on the bed.

I don't recognize myself in the mirror, but I imagine that I do look like someone Jesika would be friends with now. Where before I was mousy and plain, I'm now sparkling with polished perfection. My skin has so many layers of makeup, I look practically airbrushed. If I were one for showing my real face on social media, this would be the time for a selfie.

Instead, I focus on the bedazzled spaghetti strap that sparkles with crystals and rhinestones. After I left Jesika this morning, I went right to the nearest clothing store on Michigan Avenue and swiped my card for a glamorous little black Zara dress. It's fitted with just a little sparkle on the straps to draw the eye up. I love it, and I imagine it's something I'll wear over and over.

I'm early. It's just seven now, and if I catch a cab, it should only take five or ten minutes to get to the location Jesika sent me. I could use some liquid courage for tonight. I'll have to be aware of every word that comes out of my mouth—one slipup could ruin my entire trip. I imagine the look of horror on Dean's face once he realizes I've befriended his fiancée. It makes me laugh to myself. I'd love to be a fly on the wall at that moment; seeing Dean suffer sounds like just the right kind of revenge I need to heal. I practically snort-laugh as I imagine myself relaying this very story to my therapist and asking her if it's the kind of healing she had in mind.

Nervous energy consumes me to the point of distraction, so I

THE INFLUENCER

decide a change of scenery is required. A minute later, I'm descending in the elevator to the lobby, smiling sweetly at the bellhop who delivered my suitcase to my room when I checked in, and then hitting the sidewalk on Michigan Avenue. I lose myself in a wave of people, then turn at the first cross street to head west. The spring wind carries a chill I hadn't expected, and I regret not bringing a sweater to cover my shoulders on this walk. If it were any colder, I'd hail a cab, but as it is, the wind is just enough to threaten to take my breath away and keep my feet moving quickly.

The energy of the city brings a smile to my face, and it isn't long before I'm nearing my destination, a tucked-away-from-everything little speakeasy named Brando's with a decadent art deco style. Jesika has good taste. This is just the kind of place that I would visit back in LA. It's Instagram-worthy, from the black-and-white tile floors to the crystal-encrusted chandeliers that hang over the rich dark mahogany bar. I punch the code Jesika gave me earlier into the lockbox, and I hear the mechanism unlock. I slip inside and am greeted by a burly security guard posted at the second set of doors. He checks my identification and glances up into my eyes. "Welcome to Brando's, Shae."

My blood runs cold when he uses my real name. He must have noticed it on my driver's license. A rush of gratitude swells inside of me when I realize how lucky I am that Jesika and I didn't arrive at Brando's together. Another near miss.

"Thanks." I choke on the word as I pass through the door.

If the bartender uses my real name in front of Jesika like the security guard just did, I'm fucked with a capital F.

The urge to turn and run is strong. As smart as I am, I can't possibly consider everything. And let's be honest, I'm flying by the seat of my pants with Jesika. I never expected to actually speak to her, much less befriend the woman. Sure, that was the

77

plan, but my plans don't usually manifest into anything more than daydreams.

Walking into the bar, I'm immediately met with the chorus of an old Taylor Swift song. A group of three women are belting the lyrics from a stage in the corner as the crowd sings and cheers along with them. I didn't expect to find a casual karaoke bar inside an elegant speakeasy, but the joyous energy of the crowd seems to seep into my bones. I find myself humming along to the music as I tuck myself into a corner seat at the bar.

"What can I get ya, dear?" A handsome bartender with gauges in both earlobes leans on the bar and addresses me. I make a move to pull my identification out of my wallet to show him when he holds up a hand. "No one under twenty-one allowed. If Joey is doing his job at the front door, I don't need to see it."

"Oh." I release a breath of relief. "Well—" I glance at the cocktail menu written on a chalkboard above the bar "—I'll try the vodka lemon spritz."

"Great choice." The bartender gets to work making my drink, and I take a moment to soak in my surroundings. Lots of young working professionals are crowded into a corner booth near the stage, some couples are huddled together at tables, and a slew of singles are chatting at the opposite corner of the bar. A group of men about my age are talking and laughing, and I watch them, noticing how they interact so easily. Men fascinate me, their ability to live so much of their lives on the surface, while I'm always knee-deep in some negative emotion or another. I wish I had the ease to compartmentalize all the darkness and only exist in the light. I don't have it in me, though. I'm just not mapped for happiness in the same way others are.

One guy turns then, as if he can sense my eyes on them.

He catches my gaze, and his grin twitches sideways for a moment. The longer he looks, the more his grin deepens. My cheeks heat with the attention. I've never flirted with anyone at a bar before. What's the appropriate reaction here? Am I interested in this man? A diamond stud in each ear and arms decorated in tattoos are enough to indicate that he would be worlds apart from what I've known. Dean is straitlaced, every bit the businessman.

This guy exudes urban street style and is devastatingly handsome.

Just then, my phone vibrates with a text message.

Hey, babe! I've been sick off and on since I saw you this morning. Was hoping I'd feel better by now, but unfortunately, I don't think I'm fit for company. So sorry to cancel on you so late—let's reschedule soon! xo, J

My face falls.

Jesika has just stood me up. All the makeup and the Zara dress and the anxiety about getting ID'd in front of this woman were all for nothing.

I take a few deep breaths and then type out a quick reply.

No worries! Feel better soon. xoxo

With annoyance bubbling through my veins, I shove my phone into my bag and then move to push myself away from the bar to get the hell out of here.

"Leaving already?" I turn to find *him*. The guy from across the bar. He's even more attractive in person, eyes shining with amusement as he sits down in the chair next to me.

"Oh. Hi." I'm frozen, no words running through my mind.

"Hi." He nods to my bag. "Get bad news just now?"

"Um." I press my lips together, wondering what to say. "My friend isn't feeling well. She canceled our plans."

"Oh shit. Well, can't let a good night go to waste."

"Yeah." I avert my eyes, already feeling like the conversation has run its course. The bartender passes me my drink then.

"Wanna start a tab?" he asks.

"No, that's okay. Thanks."

"Put it on my tab, wouldya?" the companion at my shoulder interjects.

"No, no, that's okay."

"Please, you've just been stood up. We've got to make this night worth it somehow."

"Oh." All I can think is how much I want to leave. My pajamas and a bottle of wine are calling me. I imagine cuddling up on the chaise lounge with my binoculars and seeing if I can spy Jesika and Dean through the window.

"I'm Bishop."

Chapter Fifteen

My companion thrusts a hand out with a smile, and I'm immediately taken with the licks of ink that wrap around his wrist and bleed down his fingers.

"Maya," I say without thinking. The vodka lemon spritz is smooth. So smooth, it's dangerous. Kind of like Bishop.

"Well, I think I'll call you 'beautiful.'"

"Charming." I snort-laugh. "And original."

He squints. "You're a tough nut to crack, aren't you?"

"Only until you get to know me."

"Naw." He shakes his head. "I can tell. You keep things close. I bet you have a lot of secrets."

"Secrets?" I'm suddenly feeling prickly. "I don't know you— am I supposed to divulge my deepest and darkest to a stranger at a bar?"

"Ooh, stranger? That hurts. The fact that you don't like what I've just said tells me all I need to know."

"Really?" I retort.

"Hey!" Bishops throws his hands in the air with a laugh. "Game recognizes game! I meant no harm."

"Sure. You probably pick up a different woman every night of the week."

"Well, not every night," he muses.

The vodka finally seems to be working its magic. Tension has been replaced by lighthearted banter. Maybe this is the key to happiness—vodka and flirting with strangers. I suddenly regret that I didn't do more of this before I married Dean. I went from my parents' house to Dean's without a break in between, and it's taken until now to realize just what I missed out on.

"I've never met anyone like you."

"Like me?" I laugh. "What's that mean?"

"You know...*smart.*"

"We've exchanged a dozen words between us. We're hardly friends," I point out.

"*Not yet.*" Bishop proceeds to ask me a flurry of questions—if I'm from around here and what neighborhood I'm staying in. He gives me restaurant recommendations and asks me what I do for work. I tell him as many half-truths as I can muster before he orders another round for us. The longer I sit listening to his velvety voice, the more it intoxicates me as much as the vodka. He's not my type, not by a long shot, but then, I'm definitely not his type either. Where he is all rough edges covered in a thin layer of ink and charm, I'm poised and elegant and well-spoken. My every word measured. I'm surprised to find we have a lot to talk about, and soon, I've forgotten that I was even stood up by Jesika.

Bishop is confident, the way he holds himself, with his arm brushing against mine now and again as we talk...I find myself wondering what it would be like to kiss his full lips.

It doesn't take me long to find out. By the time we've finished our third round of drinks, he's pressing his lips to mine in a quick, stolen kiss that makes my heart beat double time. I've never been kissed at a bar by a stranger, and the feeling it evokes in my body is addicting.

"I should be going soon," I murmur between breathless kisses. He has his fingers woven into my hair at the base of my neck, dark eyes trained on me.

"Let me walk you back to your hotel."

"Okay," I say without thinking of any of the repercussions. For the first time in my life, I know what it feels like to think with my heart and not my head. Bishop pays his tab, and I offer to pay him for my drinks. He shakes his head in a firm no and then locks our hands and escorts me to the door. The security guard who checked my ID on the way in nods as we depart, and I pray he doesn't call me by my name.

He doesn't, and within the next minute, we're walking hand in hand down the sidewalk. I'm more than a little drunk and wobbling on my heels, but Bishop's support is strong as he guides me down streets and alleyways until we come out in front of Millennium Park. Once we finally stop in front of my hotel, I feel like Bishop is an old friend I can trust with anything —or almost anything.

"Come upstairs?" I hum against his lips.

His embrace tightens around me for a moment, and a soft growl escapes his throat. It's the sexiest thing I've ever heard, and right now, all I can think about are his hands on my skin and his lips trailing kisses along mine.

"Does this make us *friends* now?" I can hear the amusement in his question.

"Maybe." I flirt, then pull away to enter the hotel.

Bishop's fingers are locked with mine as we pass through the lobby. Once we're in the elevator and the doors close, he presses me against the wall with his body, and his hands are cupping my cheeks as he kisses me like he's never kissed me before. He steals the breath from my lungs when he slips one hand under the strap of my little black Zara dress, and he moves it aside to plant soft kisses along the line of my shoulder and collarbone. He's romancing me, and whether he's still here in the morning or not doesn't matter to me, because right now, here with him, feels so very right.

When the elevator dings at the top floor, we exit with our lips attached. I walk backward down the hallway as I fumble for my room key in my bag without breaking contact with this gorgeous man. He finally releases me from his all-consuming kisses and helps me dig through my bag until the little white keycard is located. I swipe it at the lock, and a tiny green light illuminates the box. Bishop grasps the handle and shoves, backing me into the hotel room as his greedy hands find my body again.

Every piece of me feels on fire. Bishop is not a man I would have dated before. I still wouldn't choose him because he's just not boyfriend material—the way his hands move across my body and his lips demand all of my attention is indication enough that he's had a lot of practice pleasuring a woman. Even the way he dresses makes him look like a player. But something about him is so fun, I've forgotten all my sense and why I'm even here in the first place in the pursuit of the attention he's paying me at this moment.

"Can I undress you?" he asks like a proper gentleman.

I nod, eyes transfixed on his.

"Good girl." He grins, then dips his head to suck at the tender skin of my neck. A groan falls from my lips, and I succumb to him totally. I've long forgotten my alternative plans for the night—a bottle of wine and my binoculars at the window —in favor of my own pleasure. I feel like a slut, but I like the feeling.

My life with Dean had always been so measured, so aware of appearances, as we cultivated his reputation as the top-selling residential real estate agent in LA County. But here, I am lost, and I don't ever want to be found.

The next moments move like a blur as Bishop strips me of my dress and then pushes my back against the window and drops to his knees. His firm grip holds my thighs in place before his mouth descends on me, sliding against the tender folds of my flesh until I'm shivering and quaking. Dean never did this—never put my pleasure before his own. Our sex life could best be described as robotic, when it even happened at all.

Bishop's hands are rough, his fingertips digging into my thighs as he focuses his attention on the one zone that makes my knees shake. Moments later, my limbs are heavy and my mind is drunk with endorphins as Bishop lays me back on the bed then strips himself of his black T-shirt and lowers himself over me. He cages me with his lips, moving softly before his movements become more intense, rawer. I'm reminded of the way Dean used to handle me—rough, like he hadn't had me in years. I liked it at first, but then our moments of intimacy became quick and few and far between, and my interest in him at all waned. I'd thrown myself into making Mia Starr then, but here now, with Bishop's hot body pressed to mine, I can't even begin to care about everything I've built. I just want to please him and keep him pleasing me.

I just want to be his.

Thoughts of revenge are replaced by all the different positions this man could take me in. I imagine how much fun we'd have, and then I think about staying in Chicago with Bishop and Dean and Jesika and what a fucked-up little extended family we'd be. It brings a wry smile to my face that doesn't go unnoticed by Bishop. He flips me over in bed and then lands a swift spank on my right ass cheek.

"Ow!" I grimace and rub the burn.

"Tell me what made you smile."

"No," I say before thinking.

He growls, yanks on my hair, and pulls me back against his body. It hurts. Like, *really* hurts. Tears burn my eyelids, but still, I refuse to tell him what insane idea had me nearly giggling.

"Be a good girl, or I'll spank you again."

I almost choke on my tongue before realizing that another spanking by this man actually doesn't sound half bad. I can still feel the sting from the first, and I'm finding I kind of like it.

"No," I say firmly.

His grip tightens in my hair, and he turns my neck to expose my lips to him. He bites at my full bottom lip hard enough to leave a painful bruise, before he pulls away and smacks my right ass cheek again. It burns more this time because he's landed the second smack in the same spot as the first.

"Tell me or else."

I grit my teeth, wondering if I should gamble on a third spank. An idea flits into my head, and I speak before I can think twice. "I was thinking I might have to extend my stay in Chicago a few days."

"Mm." His tongue darts out and licks his lip before he leans in and kisses me roughly. "Good girl."

His hands are between my thighs then, working at bringing me more pleasure.

"You deserve a reward. What do you want?"

My mind hums with the possibilities before I finally settle on the one that keeps popping up.

"Will you spank me again in front of the window?"

Bishop's eyes sparkle, a reckless grin turning up his lips. "With pleasure, beautiful."

Chapter Sixteen

I feel him next to me.

Before my eyes even open, I know he's there.

I signal that I'm awake with a stretch and a yawn, turning into Bishop's hard body and nestling myself under his arm. He hums a soft good morning and plants a kiss on my forehead. He's attentive, I'll give him that.

"Sleep well, beautiful?"

"Amazing. Especially considering everything hurts." I tickle my fingertips along his bare stomach under the crisp luxury sheet.

"Say thank you," he demands. I suppress my laugh at the silly dominant act he plays, but then I go along with it.

"Thank you," I whisper dutifully. I wonder if he plans on having sex with me like that every night, because if that's the case, I don't think my body can handle it.

"I ordered room service breakfast. One of everything. I hope you're hungry."

"One of everything?"

I gulp, thinking of my poor credit card. I do the mental math. At over a thousand dollars a night, I guess I could only afford to stay a month or two before my bank accounts would start to suffer. I'd have to conjure another tragedy online just to pay for my flight home.

"Breakfast sounds great."

"Good. You need to eat more anyway. I like a little more to hang on to when I'm making you scream." He pinches my waist, and I hate him instantly. I squirm, pretend to giggle, and then move out of the bed and head for the bathroom.

When I return a few minutes later, I remain silent.

"Everything okay?" Bishop fingers the spaghetti strap of the slip I've just put on.

"Y-yes." I allow him to hear the quaver in my voice.

"Tell me what's going on. Did I do something wrong?" He holds my shoulders and forces me to look him in the eyes.

"No, it's just...my ex was very *heavy-handed*."

"Heavy-handed, what does that mean?"

I shake my head, acting as if I'm struggling to find the right words. "He...hit me. Once in a while."

"He hit you?" Anger bunches his muscles.

"I... Sometimes he got upset—"

"How often did he get upset?"

"I dunno." I shrug, dropping to sit in the nearby chair at the window. "A few times a week."

"He hit you a few times a week?"

"Sometimes," I admit quietly.

"I'd fucking kill him if I ever saw him. He shouldn't lay his hands on you."

"Well, he left me, so he never will again."

"Is he here—in Chicago?"

I only nod, swiping at a fake tear. "It's a funny story, actually... I-I shouldn't tell you."

"Tell me everything," Bishop demands.

I don't, letting his last words linger.

"Tell me, beautiful. Don't make me spank it out of you—oh Jesus, the spankings. Did I hurt you? I wish I would have known."

"No! No, I loved it. It surprised me at first, but I liked everything about last night. It's just...just now, when you told me to gain some weight and pinched my side, it reminded me of something he would have said."

"Oh. Fuck. I'm so sorry." Bishop gathers me in his arms, breathing into my neck as he holds me. "Thank you for telling me."

I only nod, thankful to have someone on my team for once.

Part one of my plan for revenge is in place, and Bishop does not know it yet, but he's just become my accomplice.

"The worst part is that he emptied our shared accounts when he left and moved in with his new girlfriend. He's such a piece of shit. I can handle what he did to me, but I'm so worried about the new woman, and worse...she has a young kid. I'm so afraid he might fly into a rage and hurt them both. An innocent little kid never deserves to have the shit beat out of them."

"Dammit." Bishop pushes a hand over his short-cropped dark hair. "Some people are just better off dead."

"Tell me about it," I huff, thinking Bishop is a better guy than I first pegged him for—willing to avenge my honor and rescue some imaginary kid from harm.

"I haven't been able to sleep since he left. I lie awake at night and either live in fear of him coming back to finish me off, or me finding him first and taking care of him before he can really kill me." I pause, then add for dramatic effect, "My therapist says fantasizing about revenge is my brain's way of controlling the horrible things he did to me."

Bishop only nods. I can see I've left an impression on him. Some switch inside him seems to have been flipped. He looks angry, strong and powerful, and like he's out for blood.

"I have even dreamed about how I would do it. Maybe slip something into his morning coffee or hire a hit man—I've imagined every crazy thing you can think of!" An embarrassed laugh bubbles past my lips. "I shouldn't be telling you this. I'm sorry. You probably want to run far away from me now."

Bishop shakes his head, eyes swinging around the messy penthouse that still smells like sex before they land on me again. "He should suffer for what he did to you."

I shake my head, blowing him off. "I tried calling the police before, but they never showed up. I don't know if he paid them off or if they're just overworked and never came... It doesn't matter anyway. His brother is a lawyer and would get him off quicker than I could yell domestic abuse." I press my lips together, as if losing myself in thought. "I just wish I were smart enough to plan and execute some justice myself."

Bishop nods, his grin widening. "Vigilante justice, huh?" He holds my hands in both of his and places a kiss on my knuckles. "I volunteer to be the valiant knight at your service, if you'll have me." I giggle, allowing him to kiss his way up my arm before he sucks at my earlobe and nips softly. "I mean it, beautiful. I'd kill the motherfucker if I ever saw him."

Chapter Seventeen

I huff, tapping my pen against the edge of my laptop. I've just finished my third latte at the Roastery and still no sign of Jesika. I've been camping out here every morning for three hours in the hope of seeing my new friend. Well, in truth, I'm also trying to escape Bishop. He hasn't left my hotel room since I brought him home for what I thought was destined to be my first and last one-night stand. *Surprise!* The bastard stayed. I've been bouncing back and forth between being annoyed that he just won't leave and feeling blessed that he fell into my life and will hopefully help me get revenge on Dean.

Maybe my little one-night-stand cockroach will make himself useful after all.

As it is, he only leaves the hotel room for a few hours every evening to *do business.*

He won't tell me what kind of business, and I figure that means I shouldn't ask questions I really don't want to know the answers to. The Bishop situation, coupled with the ever-accruing charges on the hotel bill, has me feeling rattled. Bishop orders room service twice a day, and every time I come back to the room to find more dirty plates, I have to bite my tongue to stop myself from lashing out. After all, if Bishop makes good on his plan to avenge my honor, the pricey hotel bill will be well worth it. I just have to find the right moment to make the next move.

The reason I haven't been able to get a handle on the right moment is because Jesika has suddenly gone MIA on me. Well, not totally. She claims she's been sick—but it's been over a week, and I've offered to bring her chicken noodle soup from a local deli, but she hasn't even answered me.

I never intended to stay in the city this long, and then Bishop happened. And then Jesika stopped seeing me as quickly as she'd started. At this point, I'm convinced she's lying to me, and so I've spent every morning at the Roastery, waiting for the day she comes in.

The place is always busy; hipster Chicagoans have a thing for caffeinating all day long, apparently.

I close my email client, preparing to put away my laptop and take myself for a quick walk across the street to the park when a familiar broad stretch of shoulders walks in. A breath catches in my throat, and I'm left frozen.

It's him.

I know it is.

I nearly stand to greet him on instinct, and then I remember myself and instead turn to hide in the corner. My heart thunders as I think of the familiar planes of my husband's face. His hair is longer now, soft salt-and-pepper waves fanning out around his earlobes. He's growing it out. I wonder if that's because Jesika requested it. Or maybe he just hasn't found a barber to his liking here in the city.

I hate to say that he looks good, but he does. Heart-stoppingly good.

He's no Bishop, but then Bishop is a decade younger and has the flush of a reckless youth on his cheeks. Dean is dignified where Bishop is mischievous. There's no question any warm-blooded woman would pick Bishop out of a lineup of most attractive men, but there's something about my Dean. The salt-and-pepper at his temples and the laugh lines bracketing his lips are just two of my favorite things about him. He's handsome in his own way, and I hate that seeing him before me right now makes me miss him. He's someone else's now, but that doesn't change the fact that he's still my husband. At least on paper.

After a minute of digging through my bag and pretending not to look his way, I switch tactics and move my laptop bag to obscure my face. And then I chance a glance at him. He's facing away from me, and he's dressed in the same dark khakis I bought him for his birthday last year. I can tell it's them because they're scuffed at the hems where they drag along the sidewalk—they needed hemming, but I never got around to dropping them off before they began to fray.

He turns to the side then, cocking his hip against the counter as he watches the barista make his espresso. He's also wearing a new navy polo shirt. It's Lacoste, I can tell by the tiny, embroidered alligator above his heart. I wonder if it's a gift from Jesika.

And then my husband turns, and I swear he almost catches sight of me.

I hold my breath, afraid to look any closer as I pretend to fiddle with the hook on my bag. My anxiety is through the roof, heart slamming against my rib cage as I will the barista to work faster. Dean cocks a hip against the counter and crosses his arms as he waits. He's turned partially away from me, so I take a few long moments to let my gaze wander over him. Was it him fucking Jesika with frenzied passion against the window of their new apartment? I can't imagine him being so...impassioned. But I'm one hundred percent positive it was Jesika against the window, so there's no question she was fucking my husband.

The urge to go to him is strong, and for the first time, I wonder what the hell I'm doing here. I'm torturing myself, without a doubt. If Dean caught sight of me, he'd probably take out a personal protection order and force me to stay a minimum of three hundred feet away from him and everyone in his life.

Dean turns with his coffee order then, eyes skipping across the room before he makes his way to the exit. As he leaves, he takes a quick left, and I imagine him walking back down Michigan Avenue to deliver Jesika her latte. If she's drinking coffee, she must be feeling better. I think about sending her a message just to check up on her, but then she might find me a little too eager to be her friend. I pack up my things and exit the café a minute later, thankful that my husband is so self-involved he didn't pause to do a scan of the tables and find me sitting there, watching him.

Seeing Dean has left me feeling on edge. The mix of emotions bubbling up inside me is almost overwhelming, and I pause after a few steps to take a breath and compose myself, or else I risk breaking down into tears on the street. I hate him for making me feel this way, hate Bishop for taking advantage of me so blatantly, but then, I'm taking advantage of him too, so how mad can I be? By the time I'm unlocking the door to my hotel room, my nerves are fried, and the last thing I need is a confrontation with Bishop.

"Hey, stranger!" His voice is laced with positivity, and it makes me resent him even more. I imagine the day when I have the key changed to the room and I never have to see Bishop again. He's annoying, but he's useful if I can point him in the right direction.

I notice he's wearing a fresh change of clothes and new sneakers. He must be dropping by his place when he goes out, wherever that is. I imagine him selling ounces of marijuana to kids on the street before stopping home to grab a change of clothes and coming back to my penthouse. I'm about to tell him how he needs to find somewhere else to stay all day, but my phone buzzes at that moment. I glance at the screen to find a message from Jesika.

It's a selfie in bed. She's sipping out of a to-go cup from the Roastery, not a lick of makeup but with a big smile on her pale face.

Wanna hang out tonight?

I owe you a night out, but I don't think I'm ready to be out in public yet. How about Netflix and a sleepover here? The fiancé is going out of town for business for a few nights, and I'm a little scared to stay in this big place by myself.

I don't reply to her wall of text. As I wait, three dots blink across the screen, indicating she's still typing.

You can pick the movie!

I smile, thinking how genuinely sweet she is. Dean really did pick a good one. I reply quickly. *Sure, can't wait!*

A moment later, Jesika has sent me her address. I was right. Their apartment is in the building right across the street from me. I cringe when I realize it definitely was them having sex against the window that night. A sick sense of satisfaction swells inside me as the next message arrives.

5-5-5-1 is the code to open the garage. See you around 7?

Perfect! I reply. *Can I bring anything?*

Nope. We'll order takeout once you get here. Looking forward to girl time!

I pause, thumbs hovering over my screen. I need to make sure Dean isn't going to be there when I arrive, but I don't know how to ask the question without feeling weird. I press my lips together as I think, before finally settling on: *What time is your fiancé leaving tonight?*

Jesika doesn't answer for a minute before the text comes that Dean will be long gone by the time I arrive. I breathe a sigh of relief. I suddenly feel one step closer to realizing my plan. I don't know what the plan is yet exactly, but I know it will reveal itself the closer I come to integrating myself into Jesika and Dean's new life.

Revenge is best executed one small step at a time. The only risk lies in rushing the plan before it's ready.

Chapter Eighteen

"Chicago looks good on you. You're positively glowing, Shae." My therapist's smile is genuine.

"Thanks. It's good to see you." I usually dread seeing her, but this time, I'm not lying. She's a warm and caring face in a slew of strangers in this chilly city. "You look great."

Okay, I might have been lying about that last part.

She looks every part the aging, dowdy-dressed professional woman she is, but even her predictably boring style is comforting right now. Kelly has been in my life for far more years than I care to remember, she's seen me through college, career moves, breakups, and now a divorce.

My parents, instead of spending quality time with me, sat me on the sofa of any therapist that would listen. The first diagnosed me with ADHD and anxiety, the second with obsessive compulsive and bipolar disorder, the third with PTSD and depression, and after an involuntary stay at a hospital at the age of seventeen for an attempt to take my own life, I found Kelly.

In nearly twenty years, she's never once slapped me with a fancy label from her diagnostic manual. Instead, she listened.

She empathized. She became a friend. Maybe my most priceless one until Dean came...*and went.*

"Can you tell me what brought you to Chicago? Is it for work of pleasure?"

"Both, I guess." I answer honestly as I tuck a strand of hair behind my ear. I hate doing video sessions because, instead of focusing on the thoughts in my head, I end up focusing on the face reflected back at me. How higher cheekbones or a more sharply cut jawline would lend me the kind of beauty and attention Jesika enjoys by birth.

"Do you have plans to meet up with any friends?"

"No." I answer honestly, and then I think to add, "I think I met a new friend though."

"Oh?" she says as she scratches something on her notepad.

"It's Jesika," I confess, unused to hiding anything from the woman staring back at me.

"Oh..." Her tone lowers an octave. "How did that happen?"

"We bumped into each other at the coffee shop. It was totally innocent," I rush to explain.

Kelly doesn't say anything, and I know she doesn't believe me.

Long beats of silence stretch between us before she clears her throat and asks, "Is she the reason you went to Chicago, Shae?"

I shrug, unwilling to admit that she's right.

She is the only reason.

"I just wanted to make sure she was good to him and that... that they were happy, maybe?" I don't even believe myself anymore.

Kelly only nods, scratches on her pad, and avoids my gaze.

I want to fill this unbearable silence with words, but I know that's what she wants from me and like hell will I give her that.

"Shae..." She presses her lips together as she thinks about how to best *handle this.* "Do you think this is the best use of your time?"

I shrug. "I just needed a distraction. All the memories that we have in LA were haunting me. He was haunting me by taking her to all of our favorite places. He took her to the Polo Lounge! That's our place. I just couldn't keep running into them everywhere."

"You ran into them in LA?" Her eyebrows knit together.

"Well, *figuratively,* I mean. Worrying about running into them was enough to keep me in bed all day."

She nods, chewing on her bottom lip softly as she writes more on her pad.

"Have you talked to Jesika in Chicago?" she finally inquires.

I nod. "Yes."

"Does she know who you are?"

My response is delayed. "I mean, who is anyone, really?"

"Shae, does she know you're Shae Halston—ex-wife of Dean Halston?"

"Well, I'm not his ex-wife yet, so I suppose the answer to that question is no," I utter. "I have a conference call with some potential investors in ten minutes. I hate to cut this session short, but it can't be helped. You understand, right?"

Kelly's pen freezes mid-swoop, and she looks up to stare at me. "Investors?"

"Mhmm." My eyes glimmer as I lay the lie on a little thicker. "Big ones in the fashion industry. They want to be silent partners in a new vegan and cruelty-free clothing line."

"I see." She nods. "That sounds very exciting. I look forward to hearing more about that." I cringe when I realize I'll now have to find a lie about why the deal fell through—*I had a bad vibe,* I'll tell her.

"Thanks for understanding!" I grin and wave, closing my laptop before she has a chance to say any more.

I'll have to watch out for Kelly; she knows me better than anyone. Probably better than I know myself, and for the first time, that terrifies me.

Chapter Nineteen

"Watch out!" A teenager on a scooter dodges me at the last moment later that night. The momentum behind him generates a breeze that whispers stray locks of hair across my perfectly glossed lips. I huff, pulling the hair from the gooey mess on my mouth as I rush to Jesika's apartment.

I've already looked up the recent rental listings in their building so I know this apartment is way out of Dean's price range—he must be riding on Jesika's coattails on this one. I'm not surprised that he managed to get his business off the ground so quickly in Chicago. Though, his company is invested in a few commercial properties downtown, and I heard him speak often about wanting to expand in that market.

I guess Jesika was his chance to pivot like he was mine not so long ago.

Their private entry is only around the block from my hotel, but at the last minute, I detoured into a wine store and picked up their most expensive bottle of faux rosé. Jesika hasn't explicitly told me she's pregnant, but I know because I follow her on social media. I think of all the cute little things I could buy for their child. Jesika and I could meet up at playdates, and I could be Auntie Maya to the little tyke. So close to everything Dean holds dear, and yet he'd never be the wiser.

But I can't stay in Chicago forever, as appealing as that fantasy sounds. My life is based in LA, and even though I don't have any close friends or family I'm going back to, I have Mia. Mia Starr's life is rooted in California—sunshine and surfboards and red-carpet events. Wind and gray skies and snow just don't resonate with the brand I've built.

Once I regain my composure from nearly being taken out by a teenager on a rogue scooter, I grasp the faux rosé a little tighter and cross the street. I'm stepping onto the curb, eyes landing on the garage door entry that Jesika has told me to use, when the devil himself comes into my line of sight. The garage door is going up, and there he is. Dean is tossing a stuffed leather duffel bag into the back seat of a gray Audi. I think quickly and dash behind the broad side of a delivery truck. With my heart hammering, I turn the other way, moving along the side of the vehicle slowly until I hear the crunch of stones under tire tread.

Just as Dean is backing out of his driveway, I'm coming around the nose of the delivery truck. I pause, bending to pretend to tie my shoe until I hear the acceleration of Dean's car. Thankfully, he's headed in the opposite direction, and as I stand and come around the front of the vehicle and onto the sidewalk, I finally breathe a sigh of relief. That's two close calls today. I can't keep playing with fire like this; I will get burned. But right now, I just can't resist. I feel like a lion playing with its prey before devouring it. I feel in control for the first time since Dean walked out on me, and the exhilarating part is that this bastard has no idea I'm so near.

He thinks he's moved on, but I'm not so easy to move on from. I'll make sure of it.

A moment later, I find the keypad on the outside of the

building and punch in the code Jesika gave me. The garage door whirs up, and I duck in, eyes scanning the area. They must have paid a fortune to have their own private parking in this building. I spot the door that opens into the building and step inside. A long corridor leads to a small lobby with a box for tenants to buzz people into the main building. I press the button for the apartment Jesika texted earlier, and a moment later, her cheery voice crackles to life.

"Who is it?"

"Maya," I answer, the name sounding foreign on my lips.

"Yay! Come up!"

I hear the buzzer sound, indicating the door to the interior of the building has unlocked. I step through, angling for the elevators to take me up to the tenth floor. The building is well-cared-for but old, the elevator a beautiful and very slow relic of the past. It takes at least a minute to climb ten floors, and it screeches to a jarring halt when it reaches its destination. The doors open slowly, and when they do, Jesika is standing there waiting for me.

She looks like shit. Her pajamas are worn thin, and her long blond hair is in a messy bun. Her cheeks are flushed and her eyes are a little bloodshot, but she's still beautiful.

"Welcome! I swear I'm not contagious!" She giggles, throwing her arms around me and hugging fiercely. As she hugs me, my gaze hovers on a snapshot of the two of them smiling brightly from the refrigerator door. "I'm so glad you're here," she enthuses, and I cringe.

"You look amazing, sick or not." I pat her on the back and then pull away. "I brought faux rosé! We can toast to your health!"

"Oh, this is perfect. How did you know?" Jesika takes the bottle from me and, with the other hand, rubs her flat belly. "That's why Dean left late—you just missed him. I had another bout of morning sickness. He had to bring me to the hospital earlier this week just to get fluids in me. I couldn't keep anything down."

"Oh no." I feign concern.

"It was his idea that I ask a friend to stay with me. He's afraid I'm going to dehydrate and die while he's gone if I'm sick again."

"Oh." I have no words. I know I should be comforting her or something, but frankly, I'm just floored every time my husband's name leaves her lips. She says it with such familiarity, like they're soul mates or some pathetic bullshit.

"I almost had Dean call you to cancel, but I convinced him to go on his trip and told him you would take care of me. You're so sweet. I know we've only just met, but it feels like we've known each other forever, right?"

"Yeah. Totally," is all I can muster. She almost had Dean call me? "I-I don't answer phone numbers I don't recognize, though—after my ex-husband started stalking me—"

"I thought you were never married?" She tips her head to the side with renewed interest.

"Ex—I just meant ex. We almost got married, dodged a bullet with that one."

"I know what you mean—Dean's ex-wife is practically unhinged—I know men always say their exes are mentally ill, but she really is. He says she abused him—can you imagine? I have my mood swings, but hitting a man?" She shakes her head. "I swear some women are just out there ruining it for the rest of us."

My stomach churns with bile at her words. Dean thinks *I* abused *him?*

I'm practically vibrating with anger now. I bite down on my lip until the taste of copper coats my taste buds in an effort to stop the string of insults that are on the tip of my tongue.

"Ugh, the doctor has me on anti-nausea meds now, I hope I can keep it together tonight. I just got so sick of not seeing people, I had to have some girl time, ya know?" She's signaling for me to follow her to the couch. I'm thankful she likes to talk about herself so much; it takes all of the spotlight off me.

It hurts. Seeing his stuff mingled with hers feels like little daggers to my heart. I underestimated how shitty being in their space would make me feel, but I'm here now, and I have to make the best of it.

First, I'm relieved to find that Jesika is a messy roommate. There's shit thrown on every available space, boxes stacked in every corner and dirty dishes piled high in the sink.

"I'm sorry I didn't get a chance to clean. I've been trying to find a housekeeper to come every week, but it's so hard to find dependable help. One company already flaked on us, and another hasn't called back. Dean won't let me lift a finger to clean anything, but he's not so great at cleaning himself, so it's been a rough few weeks for all of us." She's giggling over the mess, and it annoys me because it's just the sort of mess that would have put Dean in a bad mood before. He's different with her, he must be, and that fact makes me angry. The narcissistic asshole has the ability to change his personality based on the company he keeps. It's his gift in business and a curse in his personal life.

A buzzer echoes through the apartment then, and it causes me to nearly jump out of my shoes. All I can think is that it might be Dean returning because he forgot something. Maybe now is the time I bow out and hide in the bathroom until he's gone for good.

"Oh, I bet that's the pizza. I ordered my favorite vegan sausage and cheese pizza from Randazzo's. I ordered a plain cheese on gluten-free crust and a pepperoni flatbread too. Is that okay?"

"That sounds perfect." I set my overnight bag on the floor nearest the couch and sit, relief loosening my tense muscles as I realize Dean is gone. I can't keep thinking he's going to pop up like a ghost over my shoulder. "Lots of options to choose from."

"I thought so. I've been starved for pizza all week. These cravings are no joke."

"I bet." I smile, thinking how I could use a shot of tequila or two to take the edge off.

"Can you be a dear and run down and get it? The code to get back in is 5-5-5-1, like the garage keypad. I just feel so weak. This morning sickness has taken a lot out of me."

"Sure." I pop up from the couch, excitement buzzing through me as I realize she's just given me the key codes to get into her apartment. Suddenly, my options have blossomed.

It only takes me a moment to collect the pizza boxes and tip the delivery guy and buzz myself back into the building. I'm obsessed with the posh, prewar details of the building, and I can't help but wonder how Dean managed to afford this place. If he's so broke, why is he living in one of the hippest neighborhoods in the city? Does Jesika's modeling business really pay off this big? I think of all the nooks and crannies so perfect for hiding, and besides, if I'm ever caught, I can always say I'm dropping by to see Jesika unexpectedly.

By the time I return to the apartment, Jesika is laid out on the sectional sofa, feet crossed, a glass of faux rosé in one hand and a bag of Funyuns in the other. I resent the sense of style and luxury she exudes so effortlessly, and even with a bag of chips in hand, she looks fashionable—like she's in a commercial. I imagine her life has always been easy because of the way she looks. When you're born blessed with the correct assortment of facial features that people deem attractive, doors open where there weren't doors before.

"So what movie do you want to watch?"

I slide the pizza box onto the kitchen counter. "Do you like psychological thrillers?"

Jesika's face scrunches with distaste. "You wanna watch a thriller?"

"I saw a movie trailer with Anna Kendrick and Blake Lively —it looked really good."

"Okay..." She points the remote at the TV screen. "I like both of them." Moments later, she's landed on the movie I was talking about. Jesika grabs paper plates, and I settle the pizza box between us on the glass coffee table.

By the time we've finished off half the pizza, it's obvious this movie is exactly what I thought it was—a story of friendship, love, and betrayal among two best friends and one of their husbands. At one point, Blake Lively as the antihero declares that everyone has a dark side and even gives a warning to sweet, sincere Anna Kendrick, "You don't want to be friends with me. Trust me."

That line sends shudders of anticipation through me. Every scene of this movie is the story of a disintegrating friendship between two women. A tale of greed and pride and passion in the suburbs that keeps me riveted and breathless until the very last deadly scene. By the time the credits roll, I can tell Jesika, however, isn't as thrilled with my choice.

"Well, glad that's over. You're such a little weirdo—I guess I know *your* dark side now," she giggles, referring back to the line in the movie. "What to watch next... Hmm, what about *The Holiday*, it's my favorite!"

"Yeah, sure. Love it," are my final words before the credits begin to play. For the next ninety minutes, I manage to laugh at all the right parts, tear up a few times, and sing along to the music when Cameron Diaz's character dances around her cottage. I've seen this movie enough times to know why every basic bitch on earth loves it. It's heartfelt, hopeful, unexpected, forlorn, and still festive. It's the perfect romantic comedy, and it's always made me want to puke.

Until now.

Now, it's my favorite too.

Just as Cameron is about to leave England and Jude Law for good at the end, I shoot off the couch and stretch my arms. I'm tired...of this movie anyway. And I swear Jesika has dozed off at least a few times. She doesn't seem to register that I'm growing antsy, and since she never managed to take me on a tour of the place, I'm left to my own devices to find the bathroom. I wander down a long hallway, opening every door cautiously as I search. I've found a guest bedroom stacked with boxes, a half bathroom for guests, and then the holy grail—the walk-in closet and primary suite with attached bath. The space is beautiful, luxurious floor-to-ceiling windows dominating an entire wall. The very same wall of windows that I watched them make love against last week.

The king bed is piled with a cotton duvet and winter-white pillows that make me want to flop onto it and roll around. I step deeper into their private space, admiring the extra-high ceilings and flecks of gold leaf in the vintage teal wallpaper. It's probably the most beautiful bedroom I've ever been in. This entire apartment rivals any space Dean and I have ever lived in. I choke down the envy as I enter the en suite bathroom; the modern tub looks like something out of *Architectural Digest,* and the his-and-hers sinks are luxe copper bowl shapes that look like they would be a pleasure to wash my hands in. Everything here is so elevated and would fit perfectly into Mia Starr's life. I have half a mind to start snapping photos, but then I think it would look weird if I were caught. So instead, I beeline for the medicine cabinet.

I laugh out loud when I realize what's been keeping old Dean alive these days. He has the medicine cabinet of an old man. A bottle of little blue pills sits front and center on the shelf, followed by high cholesterol medicine, testosterone replacement, and his usual SSRI's. Dean has changed 180 degrees, and now I have the answer why. How easy it would be to switch out one of these little pills for something far worse. The control I suddenly have over his life is intoxicating. Revenge is closer than ever, and I have multiple avenues to achieve my goals. And I still have Bishop sitting in my hotel room, ready and willing to do whatever I say. I have everyone eating out of my palm, just like I've always wanted—and soon, I'll have Dean too.

Soon, Dean will be wishing he'd never said goodbye.

Chapter Twenty

"Dean's been acting weird lately." Jesika is twirling a piece of gum around her finger later that night.

We're sitting face-to-face, my legs are crossed, and I'm blowing a bubble as she speaks. I let her words linger as I wait for the bubble to pop. "Oh yeah?"

She doesn't reply audibly, but she nods and then swipes at a tear.

"Do you think he's weirded out by the pregnancy?" I ask, fully aware of what I've just done. *Aim. Shoot. Bull's-eye.* She winces once and brings her hands to her stomach. It takes everything in me to suppress a smile. She chews her gum thoughtfully as she watches the end credits roll on *The Family Stone,* our second romantic comedy of the night.

"Maybe I'm just being emotional."

"Is he being distant?" I inquire.

"He hasn't touched me in almost a week. That's not like him. Maybe he's just busy with work, but it seems like since I told him about the baby, he's just been so...*not* into me."

Can you blame him? She's been a sick mess, on top of being

hormonal and her usual spoiled and demanding self, *so I assume,* the bloom is probably off the rose for Dean Halston.

"You have been sick," I remind her.

She nods, wiping another tear with a newly acquired tissue.

"More faux rosé?" I offer, and she only shakes her head. I pour the rest into my glass and wish I could suddenly be back at my hotel room getting fucked by Bishop against my own window right now. It's after midnight, and I wonder what exactly Bishop has been up to since I've been gone. I'd like to send him a text and ask just for the sake of curiosity, but that's not really the kind of relationship we have.

My phone buzzes with an incoming text then.

Comin' home tonight?

It's Bishop. I open the message screen, thankful for the distraction.

Not sure. Miss me?

My message hangs, and I frown, realizing how needy that probably sounds.

"Who's that?" Jesika chimes.

I lock my screen and set the phone facedown in my lap. "Just friends from Los Angeles wondering when I'll be back."

"Las Vegas?" She asks.

"Huh?" I grunt.

"You said you were from Las Vegas." She turns to look me square in the face then. "Aren't you?"

"Yeah, I meant Vegas. Did I say LA?"

She frowns, eyes scanning my form. "You do have pretty good style for Vegas..." I shift as I realize I've just made a grave mistake. If Jesika doesn't believe my lie, then all of the rest of this ruse will unravel. "Very LA chic. Have you spent time in LA?"

I nod, thankful for the easy out. "My aunt lived there when

I was a kid. It's like home away from home. Well, it was. I haven't been there in years."

Silence hangs still for a few minutes. I'll have to be careful not to let my guard down with Jesika; she's paying closer attention than I thought.

"Do you think you'll ever have kids someday?" She finally breaks the silence.

"Nah. Kids aren't for me. D—" I almost use my husband's name, "*my ex* never wanted them, so it wasn't even up for discussion. He was a selfish piece of shit anyway. I wouldn't have wanted kids with him."

"Oh, I'm sorry."

"Don't be." I wave her off. "I'm glad to be rid of him. He's someone else's problem now."

Jesika flinches at my abrasive tone, but I don't care. I'm secretly amused that my trash is her treasure. Only Dean isn't treasure; he just hasn't revealed his true self yet. I realize then that she doesn't know my husband, not like I do, and this will implode. Dean is a rolling stone. If he isn't chasing after his own ego under the guise of his career, he will self-destruct, and no way is Jesika going to be able to raise a kid by herself. These two are screwed. I don't even have to intervene—they're already on the path to destruction.

"Wanna know a secret?" Jesika's eyes twinkle as she leans in. I don't reply, and it's all she needs to continue, "Technically, I'm a home-wrecker." She lets the word hang in the air between us. "I never thought I'd be *that* woman, but in this instance... well, the way he talks about this woman—she's a real basket case."

My heart hammers uncontrollably. I hate her. I hate her with every fiber of me.

"He said she won't last a year without him—she's a real nut.

She even thinks— Well, never mind. I shouldn't air his dirty laundry. Trust me when I say she's a crazy bitch, though." She straightens the tips of her razor-straight hair, and the saccharine smile returns to her face.

"I need a potty break." I shoot off the couch, suddenly suffocated by Jesika.

Her gaze returns to the screen, and for one very brief moment, I feel remorse for plotting the ultimate revenge. We're the unlikeliest of pairs, but there's something about it that amuses me.

Once I reach the bathroom, I stop at the mirror, opening the medicine cabinet and yanking Dean's little blue pills off the shelf. Without a second thought, I dump all of them into the toilet and then flush. I think about dumping out the blood pressure medication but then realize he must have another bottle of backup pills with him. I could easily slip something in Jesika's faux rosé the next time I come over for movie night. If I have to sit through another romantic comedy with Jesika munching on Funyuns, either she'll need drugs or I will. I chew my gum as I think, and then the pettiest payback comes to me. With a dark grin, I chew a few more beats and then take the gum out of my mouth and ball it into a perfect round shape and then smush it with all my might under the most stylish copper sink I've ever seen in my life.

I bend, taking the time to pack the gummy white ball into the crevice where marble meets copper. It will probably go unnoticed for a while, maybe forever, and that gives me a sick sense of satisfaction. I walk out of the bathroom a moment later with a little extra bounce in my step. My small act of disobedience has turned this boring and bland night around. If Jesika asks me to stay overnight with her again, I don't know if I could resist the opportunity to fuck with Dean's life a little, but if it weren't for that, I would be a hard no. For as glamorous as she is,

Jesika is just as boring. I then realize her life isn't fabulous at all right now because she's pregnant. She's whiny and emotional and not booking jobs, and she won't be for at least another nine months. I frown, realizing I've met Jesika just as the bottomless well of fabulous fun has dried up.

"Up for another movie?"

I suppress a groan as I walk back into the living room.

"I'm pretty tired. I don't know if I'm up for another movie." I flop onto the sectional next to her. "How are you feeling?"

"Pretty great. This little demon baby isn't torturing me anymore, so that's something." She holds up her phone and angles it for a selfie. At first, it's just her and her nonexistent belly, but then she flips her wrist, and suddenly it's me and her, side by side on the couch like best friends. "Smile for Dean!"

"No!" I gasp, yanking a pillow in front of my face just as she snaps the photo. Her screen goes blank, and Jesika pouts like a kicked puppy dog.

"It died. Damn. Can you take a photo of us and send it to Dean? He asked for it."

"He asked for a selfie of us?"

"Yeah. He misses me. Isn't that sweet?" She's busy searching for her charger, and when she finally plugs it in, the screen powers on. She searches for her most recent photo and finds that it's not us—the battery died before the photo saved. I'll have to be more careful. That was a situation that could have spiraled out of control quickly.

"Here—say cheese!"

"No! I mean, I don't really take photos. Please don't."

"Oh." She scrunches her nose and then smiles for her own selfie. "You know what I do for a living, right?"

"What do you mean?" I move across the sectional from her, suddenly no longer trusting her with that camera.

"I work in the fashion industry. Photos are my life."

"Oh. Well, I've pretty much shied away from photos all of my life."

"Why? You shouldn't be insecure. You're beautiful. Great cheekbones and full lips. The camera would love you." She's typing out a quick message and then sets her phone down next to her. "You should let me shoot you sometime."

I laugh. "Maybe."

It occurs to me that this friendship has an expiration date. She's already talked about having Dean text me or me texting him. It seems innocent, but in the blink of an eye, my cover could be blown. If I have any chance of continuing this game, I'll have to get a new phone number. There's no other way around it.

Jesika's phone buzzes then, and she rushes to answer it. "Hey, baby."

I nearly throw up. It's him; it has to be.

"I'm good. We're having fun. Lots of girl talk."

I can hear the deep cadence of his voice on the other end of the line. My heart aches to talk to him, aches to feel the familiar weight of him in the bed next to me again. She doesn't know how lucky she is because she's the kind of girl that gets handed everything in life. She's never had to work to find a relationship, and at some point, she'll discard Dean for the next hot object of her fantasy. And meanwhile, I'll be here, still pining over the man I put so much work into. I molded him, made him mine, and now he's hers.

My resentment builds when Jesika turns and starts to murmur into the phone. She's giggling softly, and I can just imagine all the lovey-dovey things he's probably saying to her. Things he never said to me. He's different with her. He's hiding who he is, because the Dean I know would normally be in bed by this time of night, watching cheap porn on the internet and masturbating himself to sleep until he's snoring so loud, I can't help but think about suffocating him with a pillow for my own sanity.

He's hiding his true nature, all right, but not for long. I'll make sure of that.

Chapter Twenty-One

"Why the sad face, beautiful?"

I shake my head. "Just ex drama."

"More?" Bishop props his chin up with his palm as he peers over the mound of sheets at me. We made love for what felt like hours last night—apparently, absence makes Bishop's heart grow fonder. He might not have called me to whisper sweet nothings like Dean did to Jesika, but Bishop has his own way of showing me how much he misses me, and I'm finding I like it. I've never dated someone like him, someone so spontaneous and passionate. He makes Dean look like a wet washcloth in comparison.

Now we're cuddling, all warm and naked, my brain is foggy from all the rough sex, and I can't imagine a better time to implement the next stage of my plan.

"I got an email this morning that there's been funny business on my credit report. I checked it out, and it looks like the ex is opening up lines of credit in my name. If it were a few thousand dollars, maybe no big deal, but one card has a limit of ten thousand! He could really do some damage with that kind of cash."

"Wow." Bishop narrows his eyes. "Me too. Damn. Maybe now it's time to call the police."

"I'll report it today, but I'm sure that won't do anything." I conjure a few tears in the hope of pulling on Bishop's heart-strings. "It's just so frustrating doing the right thing, and it doesn't help—he just does what he wants and gets away with everything."

"Maya..." he utters what he thinks is my name. "I think it's time I pay him a visit."

I don't answer because this is the moment I've been waiting for. The moment he becomes emotionally invested.

"He's ruthless, but in a smart way. Where he's weak physically, he makes up for in the next-level mindfuck."

"He can't mindfuck like I can mindfuck, baby." Bishop drags a finger along the curve of my breast. "My reputation precedes me."

"I—" I formulate my next sentence carefully. "You wouldn't believe what I did to try to get him back. I mean, it's crazy, and I didn't really think it out very well. But I wanted to fuck with him so badly I could taste it, so I did a crazy thing and booked the hotel nearest to his apartment." Bishop's eyebrows rise in surprise, but he doesn't respond, so I continue, "I just couldn't sleep at night for weeks. Actually weeks. I would either wake up worrying he would come back in the middle of the night and finish me off or just torment me. He tormented me so much when we were together. I didn't want to tell you because I didn't want you to think I was crazy, but his apartment is right in that building." I point to the window. "I still don't sleep very well, but being so close to him helps me feel more in control, at least."

"Shit." Bishop's eyes swing across the room to the luxurious apartment building out the window. "He's been right there the whole time?"

I shrug. "It calms my mind knowing the bastard is so close."

I gnaw on my bottom lip, wondering if I should bring up the next thought in my head. "I...I've been so desperate for some peace, maybe even the chance to turn over a new leaf, but he won't let me...not as long as he's alive."

Bishop only listens, piercing eyes on mine. "It's time that changed."

I let his words hang between us before I finally venture, "What do you mean?"

"Men like that—well, there's a special place in hell for him."

I nod, leaning into my victimhood. "He takes so many pills... I used to stay up at night thinking about how if I could only switch them out, maybe I could finally get some peace. I know it makes me evil but—"

"I can get something to make your problem go away." Bishop's eyes sparkle with mischief.

"Like what?" I breathe.

"A lethal dose of Fentanyl is pretty easy to come by. Cheap too."

"You could get Fentanyl? Would it be...slow?"

"It's quick, clean. Easy to make it look like an overdose. It's called the silent assassin for a reason—no taste, no smell, and disappears into anything you mix it with... Damn, woman. Didn't realize you had a dark side when I picked you up at that bar." Bishop laughs. "You're kind of a badass."

"No." I giggle. "I wouldn't be hiding out from him if that were the case."

"That's a helluva mindfuck, though, following him to Chicago and booking the hotel next door."

I shrug. "It's temporary."

"You bet it is. Soon, you won't have to worry about him at all."

"At all?" I ask innocently.

"I'm gonna get your money back for you." Bishop jumps out

of bed, pulls on his boxer briefs, and then stalks to the window. His eyes hard, gaze trained on Dean's building, he adds, "I'm gonna make that fucker pay for hurting you."

"I think I know the key code to his apartment," I finally say. "If that helps anything."

Bishop nods thoughtfully. "Know anything else about his schedule?"

I frown, thinking. "He rents an office space downtown in the Financial District. He leaves early every morning through the garage, around five-thirty or so. Maybe you could talk to him one morning as he's leaving for work."

"Oh, I'll have a talk with him, all right." Bishop loops me with his arm, pulls me close, and plants a kiss on the crown of my head. "We're gonna have a little talk that he'll never forget. Mark my words, beautiful."

Chapter Twenty-Two

"I've been fixating again," I confess to Kelly.

She nods. "Have you been sleeping?"

"A little." I frown. "He's just *so* sweet to her. And you should hear the things she says about him. He was never that way with me. *Never.*" I see a flash of frustration cross Kelly's features, and I shrink back from the judgment. "They just seem so sweet and loving, I can't help but be resentful."

"Well, keep in mind how you *feel* and what is *reality* are two different things," she cautions. She's said this before; it never helps. My mood swings are big, but so are Dean's. *Conflict is how we communicate,* he used to tease. I always laughed, but I think now he was right. "So you've been struggling with some obsessive thinking..."

She's taking notes, and I'm trying not to laugh—to say it's *some* obsessive thinking is an understatement. If imagining poisoning Jesika's faux rosé with something to cause a miscarriage is obsessive thinking, then it's probably a safe bet that I've graduated to full-on OCD at the time of this session.

I've even thought about sneaking into the delivery ward of the hospital and snatching the little mongrel the day it's born. I know it's not something I could actually get away with. Security is locked tight to prevent newborn kidnappings like that, but still...it's fun to fantasize.

"Shae?" Her gentle tone brings me back to reality.

"Sorry, I'm just feeling the stress of this situation more than I expected. I thought I was doing so well, moving through the phases of grief like we talked about..."

"You're in a transition right now, and healing isn't a linear process," she reminds me. "This fixating...what's the nature of it?"

"What do you mean?" I ask.

"Well, do you think about being a part of their lives or hurting them?"

"No—well, I guess I've thought about all of that."

"Oh?" She writes something down. "Tell me more about that."

I hate when she says that. "Nothing serious...I think of silly ways of getting revenge. Sticking bubble gum on the underside of his door handle on the Audi...shoving him off the viewing deck of Willis Tower...generally finding some sort of way to paralyze or maim him so they're saddled together for life—in sickness and health, right?" I chuckle. "And with a newborn on top of it? I could lock them in their own gilded cage of a relationship in that million-dollar luxury apartment with a view. Things like that."

"I see." She presses her lips together, trying to bite back her true thoughts. "What would it look like if you spent your time building your business instead of fixating on your past and their future?"

I nearly snarl back at her. "But he was mine..."

"And now he's hers. You can't control the future Dean has chosen for himself."

I pout silently. She's right, and I hate her for it. Tears clutch at my throat.

"I think Jesika is beginning to suspect I'm not who she thinks I am anyway," I confess with a dejected tone.

"What makes you say that?"

"Despite how totally narcissistic she is, she's also a good listener."

"She sounds like a good friend," Kelly offers, and I cringe.

"Maybe. I slipped up and almost used my real name in front of her. And she caught me in a little lie about where I grew up. Just small things, harmless white lies really, but still...juggling all of it isn't easy."

"I bet," Kelly coos. It's funny, she's the only person I'm an open book with—as open as I get anyway. I don't let anyone in, but she's always been the exception. "Shae, can I ask...what exactly is your goal here?"

"My goal?" I pause to ponder her question.

"Where do you see yourself next year? In five years?"

I press my lips together as I try to align my thoughts. "I guess I never thought about that, Doc."

Kelly smiles, putting down her ink pen. "Well, that sounds like homework for next week, then. Short-term and long-term goals are so motivating and can give us a sense of determination and fulfillment even on the bad days. A lot of people define themselves by the goals they set and achieve." She clicks the end of her pen. "You have a brilliant mind, Shae. You should choose yours wisely."

Chapter Twenty-Three

"Go easy on him," I breathe, tapping Bishop's cheek in the predawn light. We're standing just around the corner from Dean's building a few mornings later. Bishop hasn't told me what his plan is, but I think it's because he doesn't have a plan. I haven't asked a lot of questions because, frankly, I don't want to know, just in case things go south.

I'm not sure what the best possible outcome is exactly, but it feels good to know that Dean will soon hurt like he's hurt me.

"I'll go as easy as he deserves." Bishop slips his palm around my neck and pulls me to him in an urgent kiss. "Don't watch. Meet me back at the hotel room, okay?"

I nod, knowing I absolutely will not leave. I plan to witness every moment that passes between them.

"There he is." Bishop nods over my shoulder.

My glance follows to find Dean's garage door opening slowly. This is it. This is the moment I've been waiting for. Tingles climb from my toes up to the tips of my fingers. Adrenaline chugs through my veins and stiffens my muscles. I can't speak; the ball that's lodged in my throat stifles my words and my thoughts. It's go time.

Bishop blinks once and then turns and darts off across the street. In the early morning light, his jaywalking goes unnoticed, and because I'm as curious as a cat, I follow him but do my best to stick to the shadows of the buildings. I'm wearing a sweatshirt with a hood, and I've got the hood pulled as low over my eyes as I can and still walk a straight line.

Before I can even stop to find a hiding place, I hear the first punch-and-yell combo land. I squint, suddenly feeling like my heart is squeezing out of my chest every time I hear the solid thunk of fist meeting flesh. I inch forward, both enthralled and afraid of what is happening. Moving slowly along the wall of the building, I pause when I reach the edge of the open garage door and heave a breath. I can hear Dean moaning, and it's then I can hear Bishop muttering, "Give back the money you stole. Give it all back, you worthless bastard."

"You have the wrong guy!" Dean manages to gurgle. "I didn't steal anything. Please, you have the wrong guy."

"I'll be in touch, asshole," Bishop threatens and then spins, backing out of the garage as quickly as he came.

"Jesus, there's so much blood." I choke as Bishop comes into the light. Bishop only shrugs, wiping at a trickle of my husband's blood that's trailing down his cheek.

I watch in horror as Dean rolls into the fetal position and moans, uttering something I can't hear before coughing.

"I think he needs an ambulance," I whisper, tears filling my eyes. I want to go to him, tend to his wounds and make him feel better until he realizes it's me he loves, it's me he needs, not her.

As Dean's Audi idles in the garage, he chokes on his own blood on the ground. Revenge feels silly now. The man I pledged to love in sickness and health needs me, and I'm horrified because I'm the one who's caused his pain.

"Maya, come on." Bishop yanks on my arm. "We gotta split."

I nod, hot tears melting my cheeks. I love him. I still love him. It's clear to me now, and it's not he who deserves my wrath. I've been aiming my revenge at the wrong target this entire time. It's her I'm after. It's she who deserves to hurt for the pain she's inflicted.

Can I really kill Mia Starr? Because every piece of me desperately wants to.

Chapter Twenty-Four

I **haven't been up front about what's been happening in my life.** I start my caption. **I've suffered so much since losing my husband. I lost more than I realized that day. More than just you. I lost a life I didn't even know I was carrying. The future we made together lost before life could bloom. I miss you, little peanut, and your daddy too.** I add a broken heart emoji, hashtag it with words like #*miscarriage* and #*grief*, and then hit submit on my latest Instagram post. It's a photo of my hands holding on to a soft pink teddy bear.

I've been flirting with the idea of this post for a while now. I figure what Jesika has is mine, and just because I didn't end up pregnant with Dean's baby doesn't mean I couldn't have. Hearing Jesika struggle over the weeks with her own pregnancy has me feeling empathetic pains. It's not exactly that I'm jealous of the gift Dean has given her; it's that...I want to know what it feels like myself. I want to be the one to carry Dean's child.

I know it's a lot of darkness. My newsfeed lately plays every part the grieving widow, but this is it. This is the final straw.

After this last devastating loss, Mia Starr will move on. I've even thought about announcing to my followers that Mia has moved to Chicago—but then, I wouldn't want Dean to stumble across my profile and start harassing me again.

Speaking of Dean, it's been six hours since Bishop paid him a visit, and I haven't heard a thing. At first, I waited for a text from Jesika—something alarmed announcing Dean's accident—but then I realized she's probably too busy to think about updating me. I thought about sending her a text myself, just a friendly good morning message, but then I thought it would be too obvious...or something.

So I've resorted to distracting myself on social media. My favorite addiction, the one that pays my bills now that my husband has bailed on our vows. Notifications begin lighting up my home screen, and a quiet sense of satisfaction heats my veins. This is why I do what I do, because the community I've built online is so strong and supportive. I'd die without them.

I open to my newsfeed, and the first post that pops up is the latest from Jesika. It's time-stamped ten minutes ago, and it's a photo of her and Dean holding hands, his California bronzed skin in stark contrast to her own alabaster shade, and around his wrist is wrapped a hospital ID bracelet.

My pulse flares, and the blood in my veins heats as I realize that Bishop put my husband in the hospital. Was he really hurt that badly? I skim the caption and find out that he has a broken nose and a mild concussion. My heartbeat pounds against my skull as I realize what I've done, what repercussions my actions have had on other lives. Jesus, he could have died.

Jesika's post is minutes old and already has three thousand likes and almost as many comments. I check my measly miscarriage post to find that it's struggling with a few hundred likes. I think my followers are getting sick of all the doom and gloom coming out of my feed lately. Tragedy sells, but only for so long,

I'm finding. I skip back to Jesika's post and realize she's posted multiple photos. I slide to the right and find a selfie of Jesika, still looking a little pale and sick, and in the background of the photo is another person talking to Dean while he's in his hospital bed. I squint and then zoom in on the blurry background. It's definitely not a nurse. No, this person is wearing a dark uniform, complete with hat. This person looks like a police officer.

I cringe when I realize there's a chance this could lead back to Bishop and me. Bishop says he walked that section of the street in the days leading up to the attack—he surmised that the only place not covered by a security camera would be in the dark depths of the garage. Bishop had this moment choreographed, so I don't think the police will be able to trace it back to us, but I'm not foolish enough to think it's impossible.

Anxiety ripples through my veins. I think about reaching out to Jesika to ask how she's doing. I haven't spoken to her since our movie night, which was almost a week ago now, so maybe it wouldn't be too forward for me to send a quick text. I've been in Chicago for more than three weeks, having extended my hotel stay, and while I've definitely inserted myself into their lives, I haven't really accomplished anything yet.

I turn my attention back to Jesika's caption and give it a quick reread. The last line mentions that the police suspect an attempted robbery as the motivation. I smile to myself, because that was the point. Bishop may have become my own version of a male clinger, but at least he's good for something.

Without giving it much more thought, I tap out a quick text message to Jesika. *Hey! Hope you're feeling better! Wanna go out for tacos and catch up soon? xx M*

Before I've even closed the message app, three little dots appear on the screen, indicating that Jesika is replying. I hold my breath until her message finally pops up on my screen. *Dean was attacked! Just leaving the hospital. Doctors are keeping him overnight. I'm so scared!*

My eyes widen as I take in her message. What can I even reply?

Wanna do tacos now?

Still, I don't reply. I'm frozen.

Meet me at the taco truck in the park. Right across from my building. I'll be there in 10!

I'm already shoving my shoes on my feet. I type back a quick *okay* and then swipe my cardigan and bag off the chair and head out. I'll be there in less than ten minutes, and all I can think as I descend on the elevator and walk through the lobby is that I can't wait to comfort Jesika in her time of need.

"Oh, Maya—can you believe what happened?" Jesika is sobbing into my ear as she wraps me in a hug. I can feel her shaking, and her eyes are wet with terror-filled tears. "I don't want to go home. It happened before daylight this morning when he was leaving for work!"

"Oh, Jes—" I rub her back, soothing her the best I know how. "I'm so sorry. What did the police say?"

Jesika plops down onto the bench nearest to us and buries her face in her hands. "They're practically blaming us for not having better security footage! They think it was a random attack, but I don't think so. I think someone knew there aren't security cameras in the garage. I think someone knew exactly what they were doing."

"Well—" I sit next to her "—at least he's okay."

"Barely. He has a punctured lung! One of the neighbors saw it happen and called the police—he could have lain there all day, and I wouldn't have known. Imagine if I had to raise this baby by myself."

"You wouldn't be alone," I say.

"I'm so shook. A policewoman told me to carry pepper spray

if I'm nervous, but I'm not a violent person. I've been doing yoga for a decade, and the entire foundation of our belief system is to lift others up. Violence goes against my religion."

"Well, I hardly think carrying pepper spray for self-defense makes you a lapsed yogi."

"Buddhist. I'm Buddhist. And it would, actually. I'm not comfortable with it."

"Okay, well—"

"I had to convince Dean to go to the police," she interrupts me. "He didn't want to. Isn't that crazy? At least there's an investigation open now if the attacker comes back." She's fingering the fringe on her designer scarf as she talks. "I swear, if I knew who the little street thug was, I'd sue him for emotional trauma. I-I could have lost the baby, this has been so stressful. On top of all the morning sickness, my system is already under pressure. Just putting one foot in front of the other most days is a chore."

"Oh, Jes. I'll help however I can. If you ever need anything, just let me know. I can help out while Dean is healing."

"You're so sweet." Jesika composes herself, straightening her back and shoving a crumpled tissue into her bag. "I don't know what I would do without you." She pats my hand. "I gave your name and number to the policewoman. She might call you with questions."

"Questions?" I nearly gasp. "What kinds of questions?"

"Who knows." She waves them off. "She just asked if anyone new had been in and out of the apartment in the last few weeks—tons of people have been in and out—we just moved in! But she wanted a list. She probably won't even call you, but if she does, just tell them what you know—which is nothing." She rolls her eyes. "I'm sure nothing will come of it. I swear, bad people get away with everything."

Chapter Twenty-Five

"You'll never guess what happened!" Jesika chirps two mornings later when I stop by to drop off her morning latte. Dean still isn't out of the hospital, so I've been taking his place however I can.

"What?" I drop her hot coffee off to her on the couch and then head to the kitchen with a bouquet of fresh flowers in hand. "And do you have a flower vase?"

"Under the sink," Jesika calls. She hasn't moved a muscle since Dean has been in the hospital. The kitchen sink is no longer full of dirty dishes, thanks to me, and I've also swept and mopped the travertine floors and dusted and picked up in the living room. I don't know anything about how Jesika was raised, but I imagine she must have been pampered because she takes to my doting on her like a fish to water.

"There." I drop the flowers into the vase of fresh, cool water and then lean in for a sniff. The pink and yellow roses are bright and cheery and add a little pop of color to this otherwise modern, minimalist space.

"Thank you for the coffee, by the way. I'm so lucky to have you." Jesika sips her coffee and then sets it on the side table.

"First, the good news. Dean is being released from the hospital this afternoon."

"Good!" Relief floods me. "And the bad news?"

"Well, it's not bad exactly. Dean got a get well soon card at the hospital this morning. It seemed innocent at first, but when he opened it, it was from his attacker. They're trying to black-mail money out of him."

"What?" Shock consumes me. "He's being blackmailed?" Bishop and I never talked about this. What is that bastard up to now?

"An orderly delivered the card. It says to bring $50,000 to the fountain at the park tomorrow night at eleven."

"Are you serious?"

"Can you believe it? I told Dean he had to tell the police, but he keeps saying he has to pay it or they won't leave him alone."

"No," I say, sitting down on the sofa beside Jesika.

"Crazy, right? It's like an action movie."

"Or a nightmare."

Jesika nods, taking another drink of her coffee. "I can't wait to have him home. It's not the same without him."

"I bet," I huff. My mind is a blur with all the thoughts running through it. I'm resentful that it's come to this, bitter that I've involved someone else in my revenge plot and now they've gone rogue. I can't control my husband or Jesika—and least of all Bishop. He's the true wild card, and now he's become a liability. At least he doesn't know my real name, but he can tell the police exactly where to find me if he decides to flip on me.

"You feeling okay? You look a little pale? Maybe I gave you my flu from last week. Oh no, now I'll be the one taking care of you." She chuckles with the absurdity of it.

"I'm fine. I think this coffee is just hitting me extra hard this morning." I cover my mouth as if I might be sick and then rush off to the bathroom just for the escape. For as self-involved as she is, Jesika is still more observant than I gave her credit for.

I freshen myself up in the mirror for a moment, opening the medicine cabinet once to glance at Dean's prescriptions again. They're all gone—every last bottle that was there is missing. I imagine he has all of them at the hospital, other than his magic little blue pills, which were flushed down the toilet, thanks to me.

I have to get control of this situation. I need to talk to Bishop. I need to figure out what happens next, before this situationship I've found myself in blows up in my face. But first... first, I need to get out of here because Dean is coming home today. I dig through my bag, searching for something to leave as a small token of my affection for my lovely husband. The only thing I find is a pack of my favorite gum, Juicy Fruit. I open a stick and quickly chew it, waiting until the gum is malleable before spitting it into my palm and then shoving it deep in the crevice between the white marble counter and copper sink.

I push down a swell of emotion as I realize he is hers now. She's the one excited to see him again, worried sick at home as she carries his unborn baby. But I will get my consolation prize to the tune of $50,000.

I just have to handle the wild card first.

Chapter Twenty-Six

"Mind your own fucking business, Maya."

"I am! This is my business! Or have you forgotten? This guy isn't just your next hustle, this is my ex. This is personal."

"Oh, I know." Bishop tears the tag off a ski mask and shoves it into his pocket. "You've told me all about how personal this is." Anger pulses in Bishop's irises. This is a side of him I've never seen before, and I don't like it. "That asshole hit you. He deserves to be dead, as far as I'm concerned. A few days ago, you were asking me where to get Fentanyl to overdose him, and now you're on his team?"

"No," I breathe. "No, Bishop, I was just mad...he doesn't deserve to be dead. That's a little dramatic, even for you."

"He's scum. He gives men a bad name. It would be a pleasure to wipe him off the earth."

"He does?" I cringe, realizing I've painted this picture of Dean, and it's not entirely accurate.

"It's too late to stop this now. My ass is on the line."

"Just drop it. We don't need the money. I don't need the

money. I have a business, let's just forget this ever happened," I plead.

"No can do, kid." Bishop winks, then turns the handle on the hotel door and is stalking out of the room before I can say another word.

"Bishop!" Against my better judgment, I follow him. "Wait for me!"

"You're not involved in this, Maya. Just wait for me to get back. It's safer this way."

"Please don't hurt him. Please, Bishop." I catch up to him in the hallway. "I can't put this in the past if I have to worry about you getting arrested."

"I'm not going to get arrested. Please. Don't underestimate me again, beautiful."

"Please just come back to bed."

"Got a date, babe. Chin up, I promise not to hurt him...*too much.*"

"Bishop..." We're walking across the lobby now, and the night manager catches my eye and nods.

"Stay back, Maya. If you know what's good for you, listen to me for once." Bishop holds up a hand so I don't follow him.

I only nod, knowing it's all out of my hands now. Whatever happens next is on Bishop.

He waves me back inside before he crosses Michigan Avenue and heads into the park. Just as he's out of sight, I follow him.

Chapter Twenty-Seven

"Hey! Hey!" I hear the shouting and I want to run to the noise, but I don't trust anything about this. I don't know who exactly Bishop has connections with in this city, and I don't want to find out.

"Stop! Let go of me!" The shouting is closer now, and before I break out into the open and reveal myself, I freeze behind a giant tree and listen.

I can hear people moving on the path and low, murmuring voices, but I can't see them in the dark. I wait long moments, expecting to see either Dean or Bishop move into the moonlight that illuminates the fountain, but nothing happens. It's as if the scene dissolved before it even started.

Like Bishop walked into a setup.

Fear thickens the blood in my veins, and my heartbeat slows to near death. I have a flash of a moment where I feel bad for Bishop, but then I realize it's his fault he went rogue. I recommended against it. And still, I might go down for it.

I have to get out of here.

It takes me exactly three steps to realize that I can't go back to my hotel, though. I should have known not to trust a guy like that—smooth talkers who charm the pants off girls at bars cannot be relied on in dark times. Bishop thought I was an easy hustle, a chance to make quick cash.

I spend the next hour wandering around the city. I avoid the few police cars I come across, cut across Wacker and wander along the river until my feet hurt and I'm hungry and I'm too tired to care about anything. By the time I finally decide to head back to the hotel, I'm distracted by thoughts of Jesika and Dean's relationship—how he's more affectionate and loving with her.

My feet move on instinct, and maybe it's because I'm so tired, nearly delusional with exhaustion, I find myself at the entrance of Jesika and Dean's building. I punch in the code to open their garage door as if it's just another morning and I'm delivering coffee to my friend. I hesitate for long moments, hand on the doorknob that leads into the inner sanctum of the old building. I'm allowed to be here. I'm not trespassing, far from it —Jesika gave me the codes to get in. I step over the threshold of the door and find myself in the main lobby of the building.

Normally, this is where I would either punch in the second code—which is the same as the first because Jesika wouldn't know safety if it bit her in the ass—or turn around and leave. I check the time on my phone, finding that it's after one in the morning. I walked farther than I thought. My body yearns for a bed. I want to forget this night ever happened, but I'm so close to touching the flame, it's as if I can't resist.

Feeling compelled by something I can't quite understand, I punch in the first number to Jesika and Dean's apartment. And then the second number. And finally, the third and fourth. The soft buzz of the door unlocking is familiar, and a second later, I'm stepping into the main hallway of the building. From here, I only need to take the elevator up to the tenth floor, and then I'm in. Dean is probably snoring so loudly he wouldn't hear the door, and Jesika has been so worried and exhausted with Dean's accident and the pregnancy...well, she probably wouldn't hear a thing.

I have no good justification for being here. If I get caught, I don't have an out. I know this is a curiosity killed the cat moment, but I'm too close to walk away now.

With my hand shaking, I press the up arrow on the elevator and wait for the doors to slide open. When they do, I step in, punch the button for the tenth floor, and take a deep breath as I realize there's no going back from here. I've officially crossed some invisible line, and from this moment on, every step is a risk, each breath threatens everything.

Chapter Twenty-Eight

Jesika's soft, breathy sighs make my blood boil.

She doesn't know what she's doing, and she doesn't understand the monster she's tangling with. I don't feel bad for her, though. She walked into this with eyes wide open. I had to see for myself, and now that I have, I can't bring myself to conjure even an ounce of sympathy.

He will ruin her. Just like he did me.

She pulls him close, whispers in his ear that she loves him and then nips along the shell of his earlobe with her teeth, each one artificially whitened to perfection. I hate her. In truth, I always have. From the first day we met, pangs of jealousy have stabbed at my heart. I knew when Dean picked out her photo on that first day a year ago that he was drawn to her. Why wouldn't he be? She's beautiful, blond, curvaceous where I am slim, and sweet where I am acerbic. She's always been everything I am not, and that's why she was chosen.

And that's why I'm here.

Dean cups her cheeks lovingly, gazes into her eyes in a way he never did with me, and then presses his lips to hers in a passionate kiss. He's thrusting into her with more energy now, his breaths growing ragged as he murmurs over and over that he's close. Little does he know that I am close too. So close.

She's ruined me, taken all that was good and left me here, standing in the closet of a rental apartment, mourning everything I've lost as they make love.

My therapist was right.

I have to kill her. It's the only way to return what is rightfully mine.

I hold my breath, ready to sneak out of the opposite closet door and leave them and their toxic tendencies behind me. But just as I back away from the crack in the door, it's as if Dean feels my presence, and his eyes scan the room over Jesika's bare shoulder. I swear we lock eyes, but I don't know if he knows it because it's so dark in the closet—in their room, period—that I bet his eyes aren't focused enough to see me. I hope anyway. It takes that moment for me to realize the risk I've found myself in. If Dean catches me, he will call the police, or he'll kill me. There are no other options.

My muscles are frozen in place as Dean dots kisses along Jesika's neck and then begins to thrust with renewed speed. I nearly laugh, wondering if he took his little blue pill tonight or if struggling to perform is the usual for them. Soft groans bounce off the walls of the room, and I know then that Dean is finished. I cringe inwardly, wishing I'd never been here to witness this. I thought seeing them in love would help me move on, but instead, it's made everything worse. So much worse. I can taste the rising bile in my throat, and I have to think of anything but Jesika and Dean making love to prevent myself from getting sick. As satisfying as it would be to vomit in one of Jesika's designer heels, I can't risk leaving any more DNA around this apartment. I never expected Bishop to send Dean to the hospital, never anticipated a police investigation or the risk of getting arrested. What would this crime even be?

Is it trespassing? Jesika gave me the key code to her apartment. Even invited me in for a sleepover. If I get caught and am arrested for this, it would be her word against mine, and with no evidence of a break-in, how can the police prove otherwise?

Dean hovers over Jesika's body and drops his head between her breasts, placing kisses down to the center of her stomach. He's murmuring something soft and sweet now that I can't hear, and my sense of jealousy is back because he was never that tender with me.

I wonder what I did wrong or what I could have done better to keep him.

Just as I'm about to say fuck it all and sneak back out of the closet unnoticed, Dean rises up from the bed and starts coming toward me. I freeze like a deer caught in headlights, my brain crying for me to run, but my muscles refuse to move.

This is it. I'm caught.

My petty little plot for revenge is over, and soon, I'll be rotting away in a jail cell with street thugs and common criminals.

Dean passes the doorway, and I hold my breath, sure that with only a few inches of space separating us, he could hear me breathe if he listened hard enough. He continues to saunter down the hallway, and I hear him turn into the bathroom. He must've left the door cracked because I can hear everything—he hums while he urinates, one trait I used to find adorable but now think is childish and annoying. When he finishes, I hear the sink faucet turn on as he washes his hands. He's still humming when the faucet is turned off, and then he stops as I imagine he's drying his hands with a towel.

"Honey?" Dean calls into the air, and the hairs on the back of my neck rise.

"Yeah?" Jesika replies.

"Weird question, but—is this gum?" I nearly choke on my tongue with Dean's words.

"What?" Jesika calls.

"I-I think it's Juicy Fruit."

If there were a window in this enormous walk-in closet, I would be throwing myself out of it right now.

"We really need to get a housekeeper in here," Dean mumbles as he passes my little cracked closet door. Once he reaches the bed, he crawls over Jesika and then arranges her around his broad body so she fits perfectly against him.

I wait a long time. Twenty minutes. Maybe forty. I wait until Dean is snoring and Jesika has finally put her phone down and fallen asleep. I watch his round belly move up and down, and I have the errant thought that he reminds me of a snoring pig. I wait until it's safe, and then I back out of the closet, searching for the other door in the darkness as bitterness flavors my taste buds.

I hope Dean feels tortured by the ghost of me in his life because I plan on spending the rest of mine haunting him.

Chapter Twenty-Nine

"So how is Chicago treating you, Shae?"

I bristle at my therapist's use of my old name. "Fine. Not as good as I'd hoped, I guess. I came for some business meetings, but things aren't really going according to plan. Chicago just doesn't fit my brand. It's not a good look for me."

"Oh?" Kelly Fraser, LLP raises one eyebrow. "You know what they say about plans."

I hate when she says clichéd things like this. It makes me feel like I'm wasting my money when I could just be finding the same overused inspiration on a self-help Pinterest board. I'm perched in the chair nearest the window overlooking Jesika and Dean's apartment for today's therapy session. I made sure to carefully turn away on the off chance that one of them starts to look too hard at their neighbors in the building across the street. Now that I know they have such a very clear view—as clear as mine, I guess—I'm trying to take extra precautions.

"I've worked so hard on this brand, and it's really starting to pay off," I finally answer her. "I thought a new city would inject some creative inspiration into my feed, but my followers seem to be paying less attention instead of more."

"What do *you* want to do—regardless of your followers?" my therapist asks. I see her scratching down notes on a notebook in her lap that is out of sight of the video call.

"I don't know. I've lived and breathed this business the last year. I can't really think about anything else."

"Of course you can. Do you remember a time when your social following wasn't a part of your business and was just fun? Maybe you could go back to that and unplug from the business side of things."

"No. No, I don't really think I'm ready to..." I frown, trying to measure my reactions, always aware that the camera is on. "I don't think I'm ready to let go."

"Well, you don't have to let go. What about holding space for yourself as the CEO of this business? Even CEOs need a break now and again."

"CEOs need self-care too, huh?" A wry grin curves my lips.

"They do." She nods, scratching away on her notepad. "Do you think staying busy with the business is filling something inside you that your marriage didn't?"

"I don't know. Dean turned into such an asshole at the end, I was just thankful for the escape. It's been so long..."

"So long since what?" She probes in that way I hate.

"So long since I had a good marriage. I forgot that feeling."

She nods, scribbles, and I suppress a cringe. I don't really know why I'm here or what I have to talk about, but it's nice having a standing date for chitchat. If this is what having a friend is like, I see why people like it.

"Losing yourself in business is good for a while, but if you're using it to escape something, you will burn out. I don't want that to happen."

I nod, realizing she's right. I have been putting myself under a lot of stress lately.

"So, you think I should take a break?" I play with the fringe on the end of my scarf. It's something I've seen Jesika do countless times, so I've adopted her little quirk for myself. "For how long?"

"As long as it takes for you to find your happiness again." She answers like happiness is so easy to find. I let her words linger. "I've been with you through so much—since the start of this business, Shae. And while I make a point of not looking at my clients' social profiles, I have an idea of what your job entails. It's exhausting trying to please tens of thousands of people, and you're willing to put yourself out there every day, knowing that not everyone will like you. You've shown up consistently for this brand for over a year. I just worry that your attachment to your online persona is filling something inside you that is making it challenging to separate your true self psychologically."

I don't respond because I have nothing to say. She's saying basically the same thing Dean said months ago. Isn't that why I've been coming? To fix this hole inside me that everyone else seems to think is there?

"I don't think I'm ready to take a break from my brand."

She holds my gaze over the screen, and I begin to squirm.

"I think your unwillingness to take a break is manifesting as a symptom of the real problem."

I shake my head, refusing to listen any longer.

"I think it's time for your online personality to go away for a while—like a retirement, or even a sabbatical, if you will. Maybe not permanent, but for now."

I can't look her in the eye. I can't help but wonder if she's looked me up, if she knows about my lie. She knows my husband left me. She knows the true story—or some of it anyway. If she's tracked me down online, she'll know I'm lying. I search my memory, looking for a moment I may have revealed too much, maybe slipped and mentioned the name Mia Starr at some point.

"How's your sister settling in?"

The therapist raises an eyebrow in surprise. We're only a few minutes away from the end of our session. This is our usual time for friendly chitchat.

"It's going well. Thanks for asking." I can tell Kelly Fraser, LLP is uncomfortable, so I smile brightly to make her feel more at ease. "It was my birthday last weekend, and my sister got me this engraved pendant." She leans into the camera and holds a silver locket up to the screen.

"Kelly Bernice," I read aloud. "So pretty. Is that a family name?" I inquire politely.

"It's my mom's name, actually."

"I love family names. My parents were hippies, so I'm just stuck with these trendy first and middle names. It makes me feel rootless, though. I love the tradition of people passing down their legacy in the form of names on the family tree."

"Yes." My therapist nods. "It was my grandma's name too. She was a nurse in the First World War, and my mom worked in the labor and delivery unit. I like to think the women in my family have healing in the genes. It does feel like a legacy."

"A matriarchal legacy—you're so lucky." I mean the words I'm saying. Kelly Fraser has no idea how lucky she is to have such great maternal figures in her life. I wonder now, for the first time, what my life would be like if I'd been raised by a woman better able to nurture my talents and overcome her own toxic traits instead of passing them on to me.

"The men in my family, on the other hand..." Kelly shakes her head and rolls her eyes. "My mom had her work cut out for her. My grandma too. The Fraser men are known for their rabble-rousing in the small town I grew up in. Arkansas didn't know what to do with the Frasers." She giggles softly then catches herself.

"Oh, you're from Arkansas? I've never been there."

"I haven't been in a long time. Since my parents passed, I just don't have any reason to go. I feel rootless myself, although for different reasons, of course."

I nod, thinking that in another lifetime, Kelly Fraser and I could have been real friends.

"Did you grow up in the country, or were you a city kid?" I ask.

"I was a country girl, through and through." Kelly gazes off-camera and smiles softly, like she's lost in a memory. "Ah, you always get me off track. Let's refocus on what's going on with Shae. How long are you planning to stay in Chicago? Should we plan to video call next week too?"

"Video sounds perfect, Doc." I wave goodbye and then close my laptop.

Just as I stand, my phone buzzes with a text. I reach for it, cringing when I see it's my new best friend. *Busy today? I'm bored! Come over!*

I sigh then type, *Sure! See you soon!*

My left thumb caresses the underside of my ring finger out of habit, and it hits me that I'm not wearing my canary diamond from Dean. I feel nearly naked without it, and I've taken to worrying it back and forth on my finger these last few weeks. It's the most expensive piece of jewelry I own and the very last thing I'd want to pawn, but if I had to...at least it's an option. I stand, crossing the room to my bag and digging through it in search of my ring. It's not where I usually keep it, and my heart does a flip in my chest. I turn the bag over frantically, emptying the contents onto the bed and digging through tissue packs and ChapStick and phone chargers.

"Shit," I spit, crossing the room to the vanity adjacent to the toilet. I search my mess of toiletry bags, but the more I search, the more my heart sinks. It's not here. I would never leave it out on the counter or tuck it away with my makeup items.

It's gone. Stolen. And now I know that keeping Bishop in my life was a bigger risk than I even could have imagined. Now I know I was conned, not the one doing the conning.

Chapter Thirty

I'm downstairs. Wanna go out for lunch?

I wait patiently for Jesika's reply as I stand in the same exact location I was when Bishop beat Dean to within an inch of his life. I'm still angry, and Bishop's lucky he hasn't contacted me. I wouldn't answer his call or let him in the door— I already requested new keycards for the room in case he tries to come back. The more I think about it, the more I think Bishop planned on taking Dean's money and my ring and hitting the road. I think he was playing Dean *and* me in the ultimate grift.

Jesika's reply finally arrives. *Not feeling up to it. Let's do takeout instead. Come up!*

My frown deepens. The truth is, I'm terrified to run into Dean at this point. I know I dodged a bullet sneaking in and out of their apartment the other night. By the time I was back to my hotel, I vowed to never step foot in this building again. And now, here I am. Succumbing to the chaos.

Are you sure I'm not interrupting anything? I don't want to be in the way if your fiancé is still home recovering.

I'm not sure how else to say it. I need to make sure Dean isn't home before I offer to waltz right upstairs.

He's back at work already. Staying at home all day was driving him nuts lol

Jesika's reply resonates because it's the Dean I know. He hated staying at home. *My social talents are best honed daily*, he used to say when I asked him to spend more time working from home.

Come up here so we can talk about lunch! Jesika's next text comes from a hangry place.

"Just one more time," I promise myself as I punch in the key code to open the garage door. This garage still has the lingering energy of violence. I can't shake it, and I wish I'd never stayed to witness the assault because of the lasting memories it's left me with. I was so foolish letting someone like Bishop into my life—including him was a risk that didn't pay off.

"I'm so glad you're here! Ugh, I'm withering away in this apartment. I feel like a boring pregnant old lady who just wants to sleep and eat all the time." She crunches up an empty bag of Cheetos and stuffs it in the trash bin.

I laugh, finding it easy to be around her still, even after everything.

"How do you feel about stromboli?" she asks.

"What?" Her changes of topic always give me whiplash.

"There's an Italian place around the corner that has the best stromboli in the Midwest, no contest."

"Okay. Sounds great, then."

"Perfect. I'll place an order for delivery. Although..." She tilts her head to the side as she thinks. "I could have Dean pick it up and bring it home for us. Sometimes he comes home at lunchtime. He says he misses me all day, but I think he just needs a break from all the business talk."

I can't hear anything else she's saying; my vision tunnels as I realize that Dean is still a complication. This is his home, this is his fiancée, and he could walk in at any moment and discover me here, creeping all over his life like a deadly black widow.

"Order placed!" Jesika tosses her phone on the couch and turns to me. "I'm just having it delivered. I don't want to share my stromboli with Dean. I'm eating for two already." Jesika rubs circles on her flat stomach, and I choke on my smile.

"Oh! I have something to give you. This way." Jesika gestures for me to follow her down the hallway. She leads me down the same corridor I was sneaking around in the other night while Dean and Jesika made love. I feel awkward having witnessed something so intimate between them, but then, I guess it's not even the first time.

I'm reminded of this when I follow Jesika into her bedroom. The giant windows stretch floor-to-ceiling, and I can't focus on anything but my window in the hotel across the street. I can see my neon-pink scarf tossed over the chair I was just sitting in for my therapy session—the same scarf I've been wearing almost every day since I arrived here. I know Jesika has seen me wearing it, and because I left it on the chair nearest the picture window in my hotel room, if she's paying attention, she'll know it's mine, without a doubt. I have to get out of this hotel. I have to get away from this block. I thought it was convenient, but turns out it's less convenient and more risky.

"I finally found a housekeeper for this place. Her first day was yesterday, and already, Dean isn't happy with her work... He's picky, but that's how I know I'm special to him, because Dean will cut subpar people out of his life really quickly. He's ruthless in life and business...and in the bedroom." Jesika winks playfully.

I don't have a response, because while I know Dean is ruthless, he was never worth talking about in the bedroom. His enthusiasm was lackluster at best.

"Hm, I just have to remember where I put the thing..."

Jesika lifts the top on a moving box. She doesn't seem to find what she's looking for because she turns and pushes the door open that leads into her massive walk-in closet.

"Whoa, this is big," I comment the obvious now that I can fully appreciate the closet in the daylight. There are two doors to enter, which I already knew—one entry from the hallway, which is across from the bathroom, and the other is the way we've just come in, through the primary bedroom. Where her bedroom is floor-to-ceiling windows, her closet is floor-to-ceiling luxury designers. I see Valentino and Balenciaga and Gucci labels on bags and heels stacked high, and glittering sequin and lace ballgowns and cocktail dresses—the resale value alone on these items would fetch more than the mortgage for a year on my condo in El Segundo.

"Here it is!" Jesika pulls out a small item from a box. It's wrapped in a silky white dust bag. "It's the first bag I bought myself when I cashed my first modeling paycheck. You've been such a good friend to me, I want you to have it."

"No, I couldn't. Really." I pass the gift back to her.

She shakes her head. "Really, I want you to have it. I haven't used it in years. It's just collecting dust on my shelves." She gestures to the luxury items surrounding us. "I bought it at the store just down Michigan Avenue. It holds a special place in my heart, and so do you."

"You're so sweet."

"Open it," she instructs.

I do, carefully opening the dust bag and pulling out a worn black Louis Vuitton camera bag. It's a basic small rectangle, and the lining is stained with what looks like red lipstick. I've shopped enough luxury consignment in my life to know this vintage bag probably isn't even worth a thousand dollars in this state. As far as designer items go, it's pretty low-end and not something I would even feature on my Instagram feed. I think of my elegant Oscar de la Renta gown and sigh.

"Thanks!" I enthuse, holding it in my hands like it's precious cargo. "You're too sweet, really. I wish you wouldn't." *No, really, I don't need your castoffs.* The more I stand here faking my enthusiasm for her secondhand generosity, the more I want to stab myself in the eye with one of the spiky Louboutin heels. "You're *the best.*"

"You are." Jesika winks. "I got most of this other stuff for free anyway—as long as I post in on social media or wear it to a photographed event, I don't have to pay a thing. Isn't it crazy?"

"Totally crazy." Annoyance bubbles in me when I realize I've been competing with this girl online without even realizing it. Here I am purchasing and returning luxury merchandise to maintain the Mia Starr persona, and this girl is living the life free of charge. *Literally.*

"Hang on. I'll be right back—don't move." She grins and dashes out of the closet.

I frown, unable to move much for all the overflowing boxes of clothes and accessories. A particularly glittery pair of champagne-gold Louboutin heels catch my eye, their lipstick-red soles striking. I would have taken a pair of these beauties secondhand any day, but an old Louis bag? It's almost an insult. A crazy idea enters my mind then.

Before Jesika returns, I chew the piece of Juicy Fruit in my mouth a few times and then spit it into my hand and press it into the toe of the fanciest and most expensive heel I've ever seen.

"Fuck you, Jesika. Fuck you and your secondhand designer bullshit," I murmur as my eyes trail around the space. A glass-covered case catches my eye. Sparkling pieces of jewelry are nestled in rich red velvet, and the top drawer is wedged open slightly. In the first velvet pocket lays Jesika's engagement ring.

I'd recognize it anywhere after seeing it in my newsfeed. It's even prettier in person. Bigger than I expected and the facets of the diamonds glimmer and shine in the bright fluorescent lights.

Unable to stop myself, I slip the ring out from its nook and ease it onto my ring finger. It's a perfect fit. So perfect, my breath hitches with the pain of it. This ring should be mine. Where did Dean even get the money to afford a ring like this?

I should steal it.

It's rightfully mine anyway. I'm the one who put in the years with this man, nursing him through the highs and lows, the mood swings, and drunken outbursts. I realize then this is stolen property already. As far as the state of California is concerned, the moment Dean filed for divorce, all shared assets were frozen until litigation is finished. So where did he get the money to buy a ring that easily costs more than he offered me in the divorce settlement?

Is there a way I can report this? I don't even have a lawyer yet because I haven't been able to wrap my brain around the reality of our uncoupling, but this...this is proof positive that the more I procrastinate, the worse this could be for me. The more he could hide or spend or squander before our money can be divided.

I want to steal it more than ever now. How else can I prove its existence to the court? I can't afford to add jewelry thief to my growing list of crimes, though. As it is right now, I'm only being nosy, and that's not a crime.

An idea crosses my mind to snap a photo, so at least I'll have evidence. And if I never need the evidence, I can always post the photo on social media with the caption: *the last gift from my love before he fought the battle for his life...*

I can even tell my followers that I'm donating the ring to fund cancer research. The outpouring of love and charity will be overwhelming, The thought of it causes a wildfire of tingles to rush through my system. They'll be none the wiser that it was never mine to donate to begin with. Donations will flood into my accounts, and hopefully some will funnel into cancer research too. The idea of starting a charitable organization percolates to life as I imagine building a fulfilling career convincing people to donate their money to save lives.

My therapist will be so proud of who I'm becoming.

I pull my phone out of my pocket and hold up my bejeweled hand, making sure the angle clearly shows the sparkling Louboutins and designer bags in the background as I snap a photo of the massive diamond ring. Everything about this closet is exactly the Mia Starr vibe. Aching awareness consumes me when I'm reminded again that Jesika *is* Mia Starr, not me. I'm no more than an impostor in a life like this. She's everything I want to be, and now she has the one thing I thought could never be stolen: my love.

"Hey! I'm back!" Jesika's tone is bright and cheery. "I poured us some faux champagne for a little midday celebration of friendship. Oh, you found my ring. Already it doesn't fit because of the pregnancy. My fingers are fatter than sausages."

I don't think it's the pregnancy that's making her fingers fat. If I had to guess, I would say it's the bags of potato chips she's got hidden in every corner of this apartment like a starving squirrel hoarding nuts.

"Thank you." I smile, taking the fluted glass from her hand. "Is this your engagement ring? I'm sorry, I didn't realize. I feel weird now. It was just sitting out, and I couldn't resist trying on the most beautiful ring I've ever seen." I slip it off and put it back in the drawer.

"Isn't it, though?" We toast and then sip, and I'm about to gush about how good it is when a buzzer sounds through the apartment. "Dean spoils me. I'm so lucky."

"*So* lucky."

"That must be my stromboli!" Jesika is off again, blond ponytail flying behind her. I have half a mind to yank on it just to see what happens, but then, I wouldn't want her to spill any of her faux champagne.

Or would I?

I imagine her slipping and falling in the champagne bubbles, hair weave flying as she hits her head and bleeds out on the kitchen tile while I watch. It's dark, but this woman brings out the worst in me. We look so much alike—from behind, you'd almost think we were twins—but that's where the similarities end. She's the infinitely more polished me, and now she has everything I hold dear in her fat little hands.

"Maybe I should go. I'm really not feeling well after all." I set my untouched faux champagne on the kitchen counter and offer a sad frown.

"Oh no!" Jesika sets her own glass down. "Boo!" She hugs and air-kisses me. "I hope you feel better soon. And don't forget to take your gift!" She presses the Louis bag into my hands. "Chat soon, okay?"

I only nod, feigning illness before punching the button at the elevator door and vowing never to come back. The hate is killing me slowly. I'm torturing myself, and the worst part is, I've been enjoying every moment of it.

Chapter Thirty-One

I spend the next forty-eight hours figuring out my next step. I'm trying to work on a game plan, as Bishop would have called it. I know I want to go back to California, I know I need to get on with my life, but I can't shake the need to see how things play out with Dean, Jesika, and the new baby. I've started daydreaming about being in the baby's life. I know it's not feasible, but nevertheless, I can't shake it. I've imagined what they might name it and if Jesika will be a crunchy, organic-diapers-and-granola mom or a trendy, coffee-and-chic-playdates kind of mom.

Maybe this experience has triggered my own maternal instincts. Maybe when I return to California, I'll make an appointment with a specialist and consider my options for having a baby of my own. That sounds like a project I might be ready to tackle. I could even tell my followers I used my dead husband's saved sperm to conceive our child. It would all be so sweet, but I'll have to consider if it's the direction I want my content to take—especially if I want to start thinking long-term.

Dean used to be so adamant that we use birth control. He often asked about my checkups and was always very up front with me about not wanting children. When I pushed the issue one night, he even went so far as to ask me if I really thought I would be a good mother, considering I didn't have a good example of motherhood in my own upbringing. I think I began to hate him even then, but I stuffed the feeling so far down because trying to change him wasn't worth my energy. My husband is brash and arrogant and ill-mannered, but I always loved his authenticity. Even now, I love him still. My twisted feelings for the man I married shift often, and the stronger the feelings grow, the more I feel a little unhinged over it all.

Sleep has been elusive, despite my efforts to relax and clear my mind. By the time I close my eyes and my brain starts to turn off, thoughts of all the missteps I've made over the last few weeks consume me. And my biggest regret: *Bishop*. He's still my wild card.

I've woken up every morning and, from my bed, searched police arrests and reports for this neighborhood. So far, I haven't found anything that indicates he was arrested, which only worries me more. And then it occurs to me that Bishop probably wasn't even his real name. I am so foolish. I was trying to game a player, but everything about it backfired.

By the morning of the third day, I wake up to find a stream of late-night text messages from Jesika.

Can't sleep.

I need to get out of this apartment. Let's hang out tomorrow!

Why aren't you answering me?

I haven't answered any of the messages from her. She's texted at least once a day since the last time I was at her place, but I'm officially ghosting Jesika. I guess it's finally sinking in. I would be lying if I said I wasn't sad about losing a friend, but then I remind myself that we were never friends at all—not really. The path was always leading here, to this moment. The day our friendship went up in smoke. I thought I could walk the tightrope at least a little longer, get to know the woman who is carrying my husband's child, but I'm not built for this life. The more time I spend with her, the less I can control my thoughts and feelings.

Did I do something to upset you?

I groan, realizing I'm going to have to say something. I don't know what, but I need to try to give this woman closure so she's not suspicious of who I really am. I think then to how quiet the last few nights have been in their apartment. I know Dean's routine, and seeing it from across the street every day has been comforting in a weird way. The light in their bedroom flips on around nine p.m., and sometimes I can catch a glimpse of them getting ready for bed. Within about thirty minutes, the overhead light is off, and a soft yellow lamp on Dean's side of the bed illuminates the room. The glow comforts me, and then at some point over the next hour, the lamp flicks off and their window is shrouded in darkness. I imagine Dean curling into his pillow and the soft sound of his snores filling the room minutes later.

I've been going to bed every night with Dean just like that since Bishop has been gone. I realize that the distraction he provided was keeping me grounded, my thoughts tethered to his needs and the pleasure he could bring instead of *Jesika and Dean, Dean and Jesika* all the time.

I've been watching so closely that last night, when the normal routine didn't happen, it made me wonder if they were even home. Maybe they went out for a midweek date night, or maybe they're out of town on business for a few days. Jesika hasn't mentioned this in her texts. But then, why would she when I haven't been answering her?

The truth is, I'm pretty curious about what they've been up to and about the investigation into Dean's attacker. If I could find a way to catch up with Jesika and guarantee I can steer clear of Dean...

Hi! I've been busy with work the last few days. Sorry for not answering quicker! Still not feeling great. I don't think I'm contagious, but I'm not sure. Want to meet at Buckingham Fountain by the park, just in case? My thumb hovers over the send button as I consider if meeting up with her is something I really want to do. Finally, the opportunity to dig a little deeper overcomes me, and I hit send.

Jesika replies within moments. *Is 6 okay?*

Perfect! I reply and then toss my phone on the bed. It's only three, so I have some time on my hands, and I think I'm going to use it booking my next hotel. I'll consider this my goodbye to Jesika, and maybe I'll even explain that I have some business in New York—or heck, even Paris. She doesn't know the details of my life. I've been very careful not to reveal anything that could make her suspicious or track her back to me. And funny, now that I think about it, my new friend hasn't even asked much about my life. She's always been forthcoming about hers but is too self-involved to ask a thing about me.

Heh. I smirk. Maybe she and Dean are a perfect pairing after all.

I spend the next two and a half hours researching luxury hotels around Lake Tahoe. I've never been there and have always wanted to go, and while I'm not a skier, I've always wanted to try it. And the best part, Dean would never suspect me there. I need to find myself in exactly the place no one who knows me would ever expect. Besides, I think Tahoe is a trendier setting for my brand. The last four weeks in Chicago have been mostly a bust, and I'm finding myself getting bored with Dean's droll life now anyway.

I've already booked a flight for tomorrow, and I've updated my hotel reservation online to reflect a checkout exactly forty-eight hours after my check-in in Tahoe. It gives me more than enough time to get there, get settled, and then lie low for a few days. Bishop can sing like a fucking canary, and even if the police come searching for me, I'll be long gone.

Just as I'm wrapping my new black scarf around my neck, eager to say my goodbyes to Jesika at the park and maybe grab a latte while I'm at it, I catch a flash of something in Jesika's bedroom window.

I instantly pull out the binoculars and press them to the window.

"No fucking way." I gasp. "That fucking traitor."

I drop the binoculars on the side table as anxiety washes over me. I'm ninety-nine percent sure of what I've just seen. Jesika in her bedroom, probably getting ready for our meetup, but she wasn't alone. And it wasn't Dean with her. I'm sure, almost positive, that someone in a dark uniform was in there with her. Someone with a ponytail. Could it be the new house-keeper? Maybe. But just to be safe, I type out a quick text to Jesika. *I'm on the other side of town for a business meeting. Want to meet at the Riverwalk at Michigan and Wacker instead?*

I have to be sure this isn't a setup.

Sure. That's a bit farther for me, so I might be a few minutes late, Jesika replies.

No prob... There's something I wanted to mention to you anyway. Can't wait to see you! xo I hit send and drop my phone in my bag, already walking out the door. If I hurry, I can be a few minutes early and watch her as she walks up. Because it's at the end of the business day, I'm a little afraid she'll bring Dean...or whoever that uniformed person might have been in her bedroom. My brain keeps trying to convince me it must have been the housekeeper, but there's a part of me that's concerned it's a police investigator...that maybe this is a trap just like the one Bishop walked into. The wadded balls of already-chewed gum that I shoved between the sink cracks comes back to me then. If there are forensic investigators in the apartment doing a DNA sweep—there's a chance I'm found out.

Oh? Tell me now. I hate secrets. Comes Jesika's text reply.

I sigh, typing out the message that's been flitting around in my head. I hum to myself, "Here goes nothing."

That guy in the photo with you on the fridge—is that your fiancé? I ask.

Yes. She replies instantly with more conversation bubbles lighting up the screen indicating that she's still typing. *Why?*

I think I saw him out the other night with someone.

Her reply takes time, and I imagine her hands shaking as she realizes what a piece of shit she's tied herself to. *Are you sure? He's been distant, but...* :(

A stab of guilt pierces me, but I tamp it down in favor of anticipation for what comes next...the breakup. The part where she realizes she's too good for him and kicks him out and he comes running back to LA and his wife, where he belongs.

Let's talk about it later—getting my nails done now!

I frown, leaving her message on read without replying. I've just dropped a bomb into her new relationship, and she's focused on superficial self-care. What a life this woman leads. If I would have received that message from a friend, I think I would have tracked Dean down and read him the riot act in search of the truth. How can she be so calm? I think then that maybe this is one of the things he likes about her—that chill, California-cool girl persona was never one that came naturally to me.

Just another reason to hate the woman who's carrying my husband's baby.

The sun is already setting as I move north on Michigan Avenue. Now that I've got my next step planned and my hotel and flight booked, I'm ready to move on. Adrenaline and a twinge of anxiety assault my bloodstream as I gain more momentum the closer I get to the river. Foot traffic is mostly moving south on the sidewalk, so I make good time and find myself lingering at the corner of Wacker and Michigan a few minutes before six. There's a small café along the Riverwalk that has charming red awnings, and I can just imagine myself sipping wine and people-watching with a friend in warmer months. Streetlamps line the Riverwalk, and every once in a while, a jogger or someone on a bike passes me. I imagine which direction Jesika will come from and then take a moment to slide up against the edge of a stone pillar. I want to make sure I can see her as she walks up, without her seeing me—I want to make sure she's alone.

As I wait, an older couple walks by me, hand in hand. They're talking about the river turning bright green when the city adds dye to celebrate St. Patrick's Day. *Tomorrow.* I've been so wrapped up in my thoughts I hadn't even noticed that the river water was the color of Kermit the Frog. A half grin slides up my lips as I realize what fortuitous luck I had when I changed the location of our meet without even realizing the river would be dyed. Finally, my trip to Chicago won't be wasted after all—I've done zero sight-seeing, but at least I'll have this weird memory.

Just as the sun hits the horizon through the buildings, Jesika saunters up, looking visibly flustered. "Whoa, that's a walk!"

"I'm sorry about the last-minute change. I was up here for a meeting, so—"

"Oh? What kind of meeting?" Jesika seems genuinely inquisitive. Her pretty blond hair is pulled into a side pony, and she's wearing some sort of glossy lipstick in a bright-pink shade that she probably thinks is trendy but really just hurts my eyes.

"Just a potential sponsor. It was a boring meeting, actually." I wave my hand, hoping to veer away from this topic. "How are you feeling?"

"Ugh, I'm feeling *everything* these days, and I'm sick of it. I nearly fired the new maid this morning because Dean found old gum under the sink in the bathroom." She huffs. "He agreed to let her stay if she took a pay cut, which she agreed to, morning crisis averted thankfully. I just get overwhelmed so easily lately...growing a human is hard work!" She rubs a palm over her face with a sigh, and I realize that must have been who I saw her speaking to this morning. It was probably just my paranoid mind playing tricks on me—after all, why would an investigator be at their apartment—in their bedroom, of all places?

"Oh, look!" Jesika's cheery tone interrupts my thoughts. "The river is green!" Jesika seems enamored, ignoring me and venturing closer to the river as she points. "I read they were dyeing the river green today. Isn't it crazy that I've lived in Chicago for years, and I've still never seen it like this in person?" Her palms grip the stone wall, and she leans over to look straight down at the murky depths. "I feel like a tourist in my own city."

Suddenly, a grim scene flashes through my mind as I imagine first responders fishing Jesika out of the river, her body bloated and fair blond hair dyed a sick shade of toxic algae green. I have to suppress a laugh when I remember the Garbage Pail Kids trading cards I had as a kid—mutant, gray- and green-skinned children who lived in the sewers and garbage cans and had violently toxic attitudes. It astounds me the things kids are exposed to in the name of entertainment. I can't imagine Jesika would let her kid have toys like that, but who knows what kind of mom she will be.

She looks childlike right now, clutching at her new designer bag and taking in the scene with a look of wonderment. Maybe it's that feeling that Dean loves so much about her. I cringe, feeling the heartache of losing him to her like a physical pain in my chest. I've been able to hold it together before now, but this time, that physical pain mixes with the adrenaline of my walk and the general umbrella of anxiety that's been hovering me the last few weeks, and suddenly...suddenly, it's morphed into rage at this other woman.

"Let's walk," I hum, leading her away from the busy intersection. She follows, and we stroll along the river. It's quiet, and the shadows stretch long on the sidewalk. I don't want to say anything I might regret, but I feel the need to say *something*.

I think about how I didn't see their bedroom light go on last night, and I try to find a way to ask the question without appearing to pry. "So, you're feeling good? No more morning sickness?"

"None at all. Dean took me out on a little date last night and surprised me with a stay at a new hotel he's working with. It was amazing. A rooftop steakhouse and bar—best surf and turf ever."

"Nice." So that explains it. Date night. "He sounds very thoughtful."

"Oh, he is. He's been doting on me, doesn't let me lift a finger when he's home. He's paying the housekeeper extra to do some meal prep to make sure I'm eating enough. He's so sweet. His mother was a stay-at-home mom, and he's expressed repeatedly that he wants our baby to grow up the same. He doesn't want me to quit modeling, but let's face it, the jobs aren't coming quite as frequently now that I'm over thirty anyway. And when I have a job that's important to me, he'll come along with me since he can work anywhere. He's excited to be Mr. Mom. I never thought fatherhood was sexy, but just thinking about him holding a little baby makes my ovaries want to burst!"

I nod, an angry ball forming in my throat.

"I think he's at the perfect time in his life to raise a baby. He's had so much success in his career already that he's not chasing that overworked businessman thing anymore. He had some horrible failed relationships—his last wife was such a narcissist he couldn't even think about raising children with her. Right now, we're just in a good place, and it feels like the right fit for both of us. Honestly, I can't wait for you to meet him."

It feels like a vise wrapped in razor wire is crushing my heart. I hold back tears and continue to put one foot in front of the other. We're not even looking at each other, but the desire to rip her throat out is strong.

"That's why I don't believe you," she finishes, looking at me pointedly.

I tilt my head, confused by her statement. "What do you mean? You think I'm lying?"

She narrows her eyes, taking me in without words. Every breath that passes between us feels weighted with unspoken accusations. Adrenaline spikes in my system, and the blood in my veins burns a path beneath my skin as she regards me like a private investigator would a suspect.

"Maybe not lying, but I think you saw someone else." She finally breaks eye contact and shrugs.

The fact that she's accusing me of lying makes my blood bubble and churn. "It was him. I saw him kissing someone else."

"How can you be sure? You haven't even met him." Her guard is crumbling, I can sense it.

"Dark hair, five-o'clock shadow, and dimples, right? Does he wear a big gaudy ring on one finger?" I ask.

"Y-yes." Her tone wavers and I know my arrow has landed square in her heart.

"I'm sorry, I didn't want to say anything. That's why I've been quiet the last few days..." I call on empathy I don't have and offer condolences with a palm on her arm, "My ex did this too. Men are real bastards."

"Yeah..." She looks up at the sky. "I thought he different."

"They always are at first, right?" I enjoy the way we're commiserating over the same man and she doesn't even know it.

"I just don't know when he'd have time to do it...he works a lot, but—" Her gaze trains on mine again. "Wait, when did you say you saw him?"

"A few nights ago," I offer, pretending to struggle to remember. "I had a few drinks with friends, I don't even remember the name of the place."

"Huh." She seems to be questioning my story again. "I thought you were new to the city—you have friends?"

I cringe at the implication in her words. But she's right, I did tell her I'm new to Chicago. "It was a hookup—I met up with someone from a dating app, and we went for drinks."

"Oh." Her perfect, Barbie-pink lips round with the word. "Well, I still think you're mistaken. Dean wouldn't do that to me, not now." She rubs her flat belly, and a sweet nurturing look that twists my insides comes over her face. "He loves us."

I cover my mouth to stop myself from throwing up all over her vintage boots. Driving a wedge between them has been impossible these last few weeks. Jesika stands by her man, I'll give her that.

I flash back to the conversation about goals with my therapist a few days ago. I know what I want now, and every moment before this one has gotten me one step closer to achieving it.

It's time to kill Mia—I can feel it. The time is right. Everything my therapist has been saying suddenly snaps into focus. It's as if I'm seeing the world through a new lens. And with my purpose made clear, I'm ready to act on any impulse required to fix my issues. Even if it means killing them.

"And how's Dean healing?" It feels weird saying his name out loud with her. Before now, I've only ever referred to him as her fiancé.

"Great! He's such a trooper."

I nod, trying to focus on my breath and not my nagging sense of rage. "And what about the attack? Any leads?"

"No." Jesika shakes her head. "No news. A random robbery attempt, I guess. Thank you for asking, though. Your concern is so sweet."

Jesika pauses, forcing me to meet her gaze.

"What?" I ask. "Is something on my face?"

She laughs. "No. You've just been so good to me. I've never had a better friend. It's always been hard for me to have close relationships with women, but none of that weird jealousy stuff ever comes up with you. You're always just so sweet." She leans in, crushing me in the tightest hug I've ever experienced.

I inhale a breath and take in the light scent of her lotion. The smell of her is intoxicating. The chemicals she's doused herself in are reminiscent of flowers and vanilla, and a shot of anger rushes through me as I realize how close I am to vindication. It's a hair's breadth away; the revenge I've been seeking is close enough to taste, and the relief it promises floods my system. I deserve a reset, I deserve happiness, I deserve what is owed to me, even if it means going scorched earth on this woman.

Dean's angry words tumble through my mind, and the shadows that cling to the buildings around me start to stretch and deepen. I feel cloaked in darkness and anxiety, the only points of light emanating from the streetlamps that line the river, now that the sun has fully set. I'm struggling to maintain my hold on reality and convince myself why it would be wrong to make life worse for Jesika. In an effort to ground myself and focus on my breath, I gaze out at the river. I smile when I realize how colorful everything is—bright-orange life preservers hang from each of the lamp posts, and against the backdrop of the green Chicago River, the entire scene mimics the Irish flag. It's all so festive and foolish.

I imagine bumping Jesika into the river by mistake and then throwing her one of the life rings to save her. The possible shift of power in our dynamic is potent enough to taste—I've spent these last weeks feeling not good enough to even be in her company, and now here we are, the possibility of overturning her entire existence within my control.

Suddenly, the promise of tomorrow in Tahoe dissolves.

All I can think about is Jesika's lifeless body floating in the shamrock-green Chicago River.

Chapter Thirty-Two

"**D**o you want to grab something to eat? I swear I'm always starving these days."

I don't respond. I'm lost in my own world, conscious that she's spoken but unable to formulate a single word in reply.

"Maya?" A look of concern crosses Jesika's face. "Are you okay?"

I still can't respond. I'm fighting the urge to shove her as hard as I can and then run to the nearest cab and tell them to take me to the airport, the few clothing items left behind in my hotel be damned.

"Maya?"

I don't recognize her calling me because it's not my name. I'd answer to Mia before I'd ever answer to what she's calling me right now. My vision tunnels, and all I can focus on are the pointy ends of her side ponytail. I hate every perfect part of her.

"You don't even know what you did," I mumble.

"What?" Jesika's face is scrunched in confusion.

"You don't want to be friends with me. Trust me." I mimic the line from the thriller movie we watched. "We could *never* be friends," I say, then before thinking twice, I do the thing that every neuron in my brain has been begging me to do. I grasp her side pony with all of my might and yank her backward so she's forced to lean over the stone wall that separates the Riverwalk from the churning green water.

"Help!" she calls out, fighting me to let go of her. "Stop it!"

I yank harder, practically forcing the upper part of her torso over the carved stone. Just as I'm about to shove her with my other hand, she wrenches free of me and takes off down the Riverwalk. She's running as fast as she can, but her heeled boots are slowing her down. Designer fashion will be her downfall. It's fitting that vanity will be the end of her.

One heel catches on the lip of a heaved brick, and she trips. Her arms flail, and her designer bag goes flying as she tumbles down the steps. There's a break in the wall where emergency personnel can rescue people who have fallen into the river, and Jesika is dangling lifelessly at the edge, the top half of her torso hanging over the safety ladder. She's not moving. She's not even moaning.

Wide-eyed, I stumble down the steps after her and notice drops and smears of fresh, bright-red blood on the pavement. Jesika's blood. My heart hammers as I near her form. She looks like she's only sleeping but in the most awkward position, one shoulder crushed against the edge of the stone wall and the chugging and gurgling green river swirling just beyond her head.

"Jesika?" I whisper. Stepping closer, I hang over the edge of the half-wall to see if I can get at the right angle to see her face. I need to see her eyes. Is she breathing? I can't tell anything from here. "Jesika?"

She doesn't stir, and I can't focus my eyes long enough to tell if her chest is moving or if she's breathing.

"Jesika!" I bark, disbelieving what's happening before me. If

I lean just far enough, I can catch sight of the tips of her blond ponytail dragging in the vivid green river water. Shades of pink drip down the ends, and I realize then it's her blood. She must have hit her head on the fall down the steps.

I gulp, moving back to her body and wondering if I should perform CPR or call the police or Dean or search for her phone or...

"Jes—" I gently move her shoulder as if she is only just asleep. Only, the meager effort I've used to nudge her is just enough to send her body tumbling into the river. "Jesika!"

Tears flood my eyes as I realize what I've done. That maybe I've even left my DNA on her body.

"Oh God." I have to save her. I scramble to find the nearest orange life preserver. When I locate it a few steps away, I unwind it swiftly and then climb down the ladder as quickly as I can. The river water laps the third rung of the ladder. I'm sure I'm strong enough to lift her out of the water and at least give her a fighting chance at life.

Oh God. *The baby.*

Dean's baby.

Superhuman strength consumes me, and I drop into the freezing water. I loop the life preserver rope around her still-floating form and then press our bodies together and wrap the remainder of the rope around my own waist. I try to heave the upper part of her body against my shoulder and then press her body between myself and the ladder. I struggle to hold on to the slippery iron. A thin layer of green algae coats the submerged rungs, and with every step, I fight not to slip.

Struggling to take in full breaths under the weight of Jesika's body, I move slowly but test my grip with every step. I'm dripping and water runs in my eyes, but I push on, finally reaching the topmost rung. Her body is heavy and slick as I try and fail to push her torso back onto solid ground. I pause, trying to figure the right angle to do this before I realize I jumped right into this river to save her life without even thinking of my phone. Even if I manage to get her out of the water, I won't be able to call first responders. And because the businesses here cater to the lunch crowd, most are closed at this time of evening.

Tears sting my eyes as I almost lose my grip and cause both of us to fall back into the river. We're connected, she and I. At least for now. Her life and Dean's unborn baby's life are in my hands.

I sob, gathering all my strength and shoving us up one more rung so we're both almost fully out of the water. I heave once more and collapse on top of Jesika's body on the dry pavement and then work to untangle us from the life preserver. When I'm free, I stand, confirming that my phone and wallet are still in my zippered jacket pocket—they are.

And then I run.

Every lunch café and coffee shop that line this part of the Riverwalk is dark, closed sign on display. Chic boutiques and glamorous bakeries offering delectables like macarons and expensive cupcakes blur through my tears as I run. I turn down the next street I come to, searching for any sign of life. I keep running but think to pull out my phone to check if it's still working. The screen is blank and it isn't responding to me, but maybe that's because my hands are wet or the facial recognition doesn't recognize me with soaked hair. I want to scream and throw something, but instead, I keep jogging.

By the time I've reached somewhere I recognize, I realize I'm only two blocks from my hotel and about the same to Dean and Jesika's building. I slow to a walk, letting my feet trace the familiar steps. The patterns and cracks along this part of the sidewalk ground me as my mind starts to relax, and I begin to think straight. I cycle my phone on and off, and by the time it powers on again, the home screen pops up like everything is fine.

I stop right at the same corner where I stood with Bishop, watching Dean get into his Audi before work that fateful morning before the attack.

I glance up, then shake my head when it feels like I'm living in a flashback. I'm having déjà vu as it looks like Dean is standing right by his car in the garage at this very moment. He seems to be on a phone call, and I wonder if it's Jesika he's trying to reach. Does he worry about her? I don't recall him ever calling me, sick with worry.

I step closer to my husband on instinct, every part of me drawn to him out of muscle memory.

I miss him. *So* much.

Without thinking, I move my legs closer. I'm hovering at the edge of the garage, just a few steps away from the man I love. I can feel his presence; something about him calls to me. I recognize that the pull he has over me isn't healthy, and still, I'm helpless to it.

My eyes dart to a red gas can stored along the side wall of the garage and a bottle of charcoal fire starter next to it. Dean is fumbling with something in his car, and just as I bend to check the weight of the gas can, Dean fires up the Audi. I nearly jump and drop the can, but I compose myself and then smell the familiar scent of gasoline in my nose. Thinking quickly, I soak the end of my scarf in the flammable liquid and set the can back where I found it. I move slowly, my steps stealthy like a fox as I sidle up along the Audi. It's wild that I can get so close to him in the shadows. *I've been right here all along, honey,* I think.

I wrap the end of my scarf around one wrist and finger the fringe on the other end. I spent so many of my waking breaths living for this man for so many years. I just wish he'd talk to me, but something in me recognizes that we'll never have that old easiness between us again. He only shows his soft side to Jesika now.

How funny it is to feel everything for someone who gave you nothing.

I tighten the scarf in my grip, lining up the gasoline-soaked section so it sits directly between each of my palms.

Dean must catch a flash of something in his side mirror because he turns his neck, but not far enough around to actually catch sight of me.

"Jesssika?" he slurs.

I freeze, unable to breathe. The urge to pretend, even just for a moment, that I am still his is powerful. I have to fight back the instinct to wrap him in my arms and take solace in the warmth of his familiar body.

"Jesssss?" his word ends on a long hiss.

My lips twist into a snarl. I will never be her, pretending even just for a moment is playing with fire. I wait for him to go back to whatever it is he's digging for. One last step and I'm just at his shoulder, my vision clear as I see Dean bent over the center console of his Audi while he crushes up small white pills.

"Tsk, tsk, tsk. I told you those pills would be the death of you, Dean." A Cheshire grin overcomes me.

As if moving in slow motion, Dean turns. His reactions seem blunted, and at first, it's like he doesn't even recognize me. He looks stoned. It must be his pain pills he's crushing to put up his nose. As realization dawns on him that it's me, the woman he abandoned for a new life, his features crumple and contort with confusion.

And it's then I remember how much I hate him.

How much he devalued me and made me feel like a failure.

"S-shhae?" His words are slurred, and his eyes are glassy.

"Ah Dean, do you have to make it so easy?"

"W-what're ya doin' here?"

"Giving you what you deserve. I always knew this day was coming. You were always so selfish, ya know?." A tidal wave of rage wells inside me.

"W-wait—it waz you? Where'z Jes?" He seems alarmed now, like it's taken his brain a few minutes to catch up to the risk of the current situation.

Without another word, I wrap the gasoline-soaked scarf around his mouth. It's surprising how little he struggles. I wonder then if I could have overpowered him all these years. Dean's control over me was wide-reaching, though now, I can't help but think it was only my perception of his power over me that maintained that level of control. I was always as strong and capable as I am right now. It just took until this moment to prove it to myself.

I've loved him. I've hated him. And now, I've become indifferent to him.

Dean is tearing at the scarf, but I tighten my hold, feeling his strength give out as I dominate his drug-addled body.

Within moments, he is lifeless. As soon as the light goes out in his eyes and his body slumps, I loosen the scarf and back away. Tears overwhelm my eyes, and my limbs tremble with adrenaline as I look at the situation I've created. I made them my pawns the last four weeks, exacted some sense of closure, and maybe got a little modicum of revenge while I did it. I feel satisfied, like an oppressive weight has been lifted. Suddenly, the rain clouds have parted, and I'm eager to move on to my next adventure.

I waltz out of Dean's garage, wrapping the scarf around my hand and punching the button to close the garage door as I walk away. Dean's Audi is still running, and if someone doesn't find him soon, who knows what will happen. Such a tragic accident. Dean—high out of his mind and recovering from a random act of violence only a few weeks ago—passes away in his car because he started the engine without opening the door and then lost consciousness.

Now, my husband really is dead, and my online persona as a widow is a reality. It's like I manifested this outcome out of thin air. The overused Pinterest quote runs through my mind that *life is what happens when you're busy making other plans,* but I *did* plan this...*sort of.* I think of an amusing *how it started/how it's going* themed Instagram post with our wedding photo and one of Dean's lifeless body slumped behind the wheel of his Audi, taking his last breaths. Side by side, the juxtaposition would be wild. I really am a black widow.

I've spent a lot of time thinking about what I want since Dean walked out, and the only thing I know for sure is that I'd rather be in hell than alone.

"Adios, Dean. Fuck you very much."

Chapter Thirty-Three

"**W**ell, *try it again.*" My irritation spikes.

The desk clerk at the Ritz in Tahoe looks annoyed. More annoyed than me, and I'm the one whose credit card is getting declined.

"Listen, there's plenty of money in the account. Trust me, I just checked it. Please, just run it again."

The clerk sighs then attempts to swipe my card again. It's only been half a day since I split on Chicago, and the mountain breeze is really everything I needed. As soon as I stepped off the plane, I regretted not visiting this part of California sooner. The mountains are still snow-topped, and the lush evergreens are a breath of fresh air.

"I'm sorry, ma'am. Declined." His stern gaze holds mine.

I shrink under his gaze. "That's the only card I have. What should I do?"

"I can call you a cab to take you to the local hostel. Room rates are considerably less."

"T-the hostel? But that doesn't sound safe."

"Lots of hikers and snowboarders. It's very safe."

"B-but I would still need a card." My heart is hammering with anxiety.

"Yes." He waits a beat, looks me up and down, and then offers, "If you're in need, the cab can take you to the women's shelter too, if that would suit you better."

"The women's shelter?"

"Yes. Fare is on us, of course."

I swallow the painful lump that's formed in my throat. "I-I guess I need to figure out something."

He nods. "Right away, ma'am."

He uses a small call box to alert the local cab company that a car is needed.

"They should be here in about fifteen minutes. You're welcome to wait in the lobby in the meantime."

"Okay." I back away, defeated. "I'll try to call my bank and ask them what's going on."

He nods. "As you wish."

As soon as I sit on the leather sofa, I pull out my phone and log in to my bank account. I have plenty of money available. Anger floods my bloodstream as I bring up the customer service number for my bank. It takes exactly six minutes before I'm connected with someone and can inquire why my card is being declined. The woman seems frustrated with me before I've even offered my account number. Once she looks it up and confirms that the balance is well above zero, she clicks her tongue a moment and then asks if she can put me on hold while she reads some notes on my account.

I agree, and then sit for a few more minutes listening to boring elevator music.

When she returns, her tone is more positive. "I'm sorry—it looks like your card has been locked, Mrs. Halston."

"No." I can't hide my annoyance now. "Why?"

"It looks like your husband called and asked to have your card canceled."

"What? How can he do that? We share the account. Doesn't that mean neither one of us can make a decision without the other?"

"Well, yes—on a shared account. You don't have a shared account. At least this one is in the name of Dean Halston, and you're listed as just a—"

"*Wife*. I'm just the wife!" I cry hot tears. "Now what am I supposed to do? I'm out of town," I repeat.

"Okay. Maybe we could get you a quick line of credit. How long will you be there? We could ship you a new card with a credit balance to the hotel you're staying at, maybe? I'd have to get approval from my manager and then we'd run a credit check of course..."

I groan softly as I think about the mess I'm in now. If I have my bank ship me a new card, that means someone will know where to find me, and I'd rather keep to myself at the moment. Plus, I'm not even sure I'd get approved—my job isn't as consistent as they'd like.

"How long do you think it would take to arrive?"

"Oh, well, as long as you're in the continental US...two or three days at most."

I imagine I could tell her to ship it to a nearby city and I could go retrieve it. I'd have to find a place, though, and then call the service line back. And if I don't do anything, I'm destined to stay at the women's shelter. Even the hostel is out of my price range.

"Let's do it. Ship it to me," I blurt. "Please."

"Very well." I can hear her quick fingers typing. "The application will only take a minute and I can fill in most of the information from your account. I just need your social security number and your current address."

I switch the screen on my phone and bring up the address of the hotel I'm standing in. I quickly rattle it off to her and wait as she types something on her keyboard. A long pause lingers before she smacks her lips together and announces that I've been approved for a meager five hundred dollars.

"That should help for a little while at least—"

"Great, thank you," I cut her off quickly before hanging up. I don't know if I've just saved myself or made a mistake. Either way, I face a risk.

I swallow, already uncomfortable that it's now on paper somewhere that I'm in Tahoe. I gnash my teeth, no longer comfortable with anyone else knowing I'm headed to the women's shelter for the night. I stand, adjust my bag on my shoulder, and then wave to the desk clerk, who is eagle-eyeing me at the moment. He gestures with his eyes to the lobby doors, and I follow his gaze, watching as a yellow cab pulls up to the valet.

I mouth the words thank you to him and then head to the cab. As soon as I'm there, I realize I have one last avenue of payment. As soon as I sit in the cab driver's back seat, I divulge that I have no cash or card to pay him, but that if he accepts a digital form of payment, I can transfer him the cost of the cab via a cash app. He waves me off, explains that the hotel has an account of comped rides and that this one is covered.

I nearly burst into tears and then thank him profusely. Maybe Tahoe will be a good fit for me after all.

"So, where are we off to, then?" He's cheerful, and his kindness nearly overwhelms me. After being in LA and Chicago for so long, small-town friendly chitchat feels novel.

"Is there a coffee shop downtown?"

"There is. I stop at the Drip Drop every morning and get my cup of coffee from Dottie. Got a great lake view, too."

"It sounds perfect." I settle into the back seat.

"Mind if I ask what brought you to Tahoe?"

"I've always wanted to visit, and I've had...some troubles lately with my ex, so I thought it was a perfect time for a little getaway."

"I see. Well, I've been here all my life. I remember it when it was just a little town up on the lake. Business is booming now. Married my wife here, raised my boys in the local school system. Can't say I'd ever want to leave."

"Yeah?" I fiddle with the zipper on my coat. I miss my scarf. I had to throw it in a trash can in Millennium Park after I left Dean and Jesika's garage, and I donated my neon-pink one to a homeless woman because I was so afraid Jesika might recognize it from her bedroom window. Maybe I can find a replacement here. "I've been in the LA area for a few years now, but after a business trip to Chicago...I have to say the mountain air is something else."

"That it is, that it is. You plan on stayin' a while?"

"Maybe." I press my lips together. "I guess that depends on my ex."

He's silent for a while before offering, "I don't mean to pry, but you seem like you're going through a lot. You seem like a sweet girl, and I hate to see so much stress on your face." He holds my gaze in the rearview mirror. "My wife and I have an extra room and take in troubled teens now and again. If you need a place to stay, well, we'd love to have you. My wife loves the company, and well, we're discreet people. No questions asked, if you know what I mean." He passes me a plain white business card with his name and number on it. "You just give that number a call, day or night, and I'll come get you wherever you are."

I nod, palming the card as my heart hammers. "Thank you. I've never met anyone so generous. I think I'll be fine, but truly, I appreciate it. I think you just became my first friend here."

"Well, I feel the same way. Name's Rodger. What's yours?"

I gulp, not having decided what name I would go by here in Tahoe. "Mia." I settle on the easiest, figuring at least I have a chance at answering to that name if I ever see Rodger again.

By the time Rodger the cab driver is dropping me off in front of the Drip Drop, I'm feeling more hopeful than I've felt in a while. I tuck his business card with the phone number into my back pocket and step into the welcoming smell of roasted coffee beans. I locate a table and set up my laptop instantly. As long as I have internet, I think I can dig deep and find some way to pay for lodging using an online payment system that's directly connected to my bank account but doesn't use my credit card. Maybe I could even find a vacation rental nearby and prepay for my stay. I'll do anything to find an alternative to the shelter or the hostel, not because I'm not too good for sleeping on a cot, but because I need wireless internet to do my business. If I have any hope of navigating my way through this, I need internet access at all times.

I spend the next hour looking at local vacation rentals that are available for the next few weeks. Unfortunately, it seems to be the end of ski season, so the downtown area is packed with outdoor enthusiasts and families in winter attire, and all the rentals are booked. There's nothing available tonight or tomorrow night, and as charming as this mountain ski town is, I'm regretting choosing it. On the one hand, it's easy to get lost in the chaos of the crowd. On the other, it takes a lot of money to be here. Anger rises in me again as I imagine the thousands of dollars available in my account that I, so far, am unable to access. I then take some time to search for the nearest branch of my bank, but it seems I'd basically have to go all the way back to El Segundo.

My best chance at avoiding risk and getting access to my funds is to wait this out. I'll go back to the hotel in a few days and ask for any mail deliveries for me. And when the card comes, I'll activate it right there in the lobby and prepay for a room. Or I'll book the next flight out of there and head to Hawaii or Ibiza or somewhere fabulous and Instagram-worthy.

If anything, this situation is a reminder to diversify. Dean set up all the banking connected to my business. I curse him now for leaving me like this...with him in control of my money, my life, my future. I should have pulled a lot of that cash out of my account as more was deposited from the internet donations. But then, can a person even pay for a hotel with cash anymore? That seems like a red flag in itself. I gnaw on my bottom lip, suddenly obsessed with creating a new persona, conjuring a new tragedy, and collecting more donations. That has to be illegal, though—whereas Mia Starr is my brand and the things that happened to her really did happen to me. There's no fraud about it; she is me. Her life is mine. I even do an internet search about the process of changing my name. Life would be so much easier if I were Mia Starr in the real world as well as virtual reality. I *feel* more like her anyway. Shae Halston is weighed down with baggage and trauma and failed relationships—Mia is my new leaf. My chance at a new life. My chance at the life I deserve.

By the time twilight filters through the windows of the Drip Drop, my body aches and I'm no closer to finding a place to stay tonight than I was when I arrived. I finally take a minute to look out over the lake and snow-blanketed mountains that tower over the area. Tahoe is a freezing-cold work of art, probably the most picture-perfect place I've ever seen. The tranquil crystal-blue waters of Lake Tahoe lap at the vivid pine and evergreen shores, and if it weren't for the piles of snow dotting the coast, it'd look every part the perfect summer destination. It's just as cold as Lake Michigan, but something about Tahoe feels more cozy and inviting...and like a better place to get lost.

With a migraine pressing at the edges of my skull, I call the local cab company and request a ride. I thought about calling Rodger, but the bottom line is, forming new connections isn't in my best interest right now. Or his, for that matter. In a few minutes, a yellow cab approaches the sidewalk outside the coffee shop. My breath catches, knowing what I have to do next. The cab driver parks at the curb and gets out to help me with my luggage. As he loads my suitcase into the back, I turn off my phone and then locate the SIM card slot on the side. I overlooked it before now, but I have to ditch the phone just to make sure I can't be followed. Using a small hairpin, I eject the thin SIM card and then toss it on the ground and stomp on it with the heel of my boot.

When I'm convinced it's been obliterated beyond all possibility of GPS locating, I slide into the back seat of the cab. The driver gets in behind the wheel and catches my eye in the rearview. "Where to?"

"The women's shelter, please."

Chapter Thirty-Four

"And the reason you're looking for assistance today?" The woman sitting across from me looks tired on a bone-deep level. I decide to push the limits on embellishing my story just to amuse myself.

"My husband is abusive. He kicked me out of the house and turned off all my access to the credit cards. He's been banging a model half my age, and the night I found out his new girlfriend was pregnant with his baby was the day he gave me a fat lip for the last time."

"I see." She doesn't seem fazed as she takes notes in a case file.

"He nearly beat me to death last month. He did actually kill someone—my unborn baby. I had a miscarriage when he pushed me down the stairs." I'm looking for a reaction from her now, and I'm not getting it.

"We have a bed for you tonight. Probably tomorrow too. But you need to be looking for a job. We'll connect again tomorrow and talk more about expectations and access to more support systems if you need it. Bed 31 is all yours." She hands me a tag to hang on the end of my cot that indicates that the bed is taken.

"W-will you tell my husband that I'm here if he comes to look for me?"

"'Course not." She seems irritated I've asked. "You're not the first woman to marry an asshole. You won't be the last."

I nod. "But he's a well-connected asshole. If he sends an investigator or anything—"

"We're discreet. We cannot confirm or deny that anyone has stayed with us in the past or is currently here. Unless a judge subpoenas the information because there's been a crime committed, we can't share your information with anyone."

Well, that doesn't put my mind at ease at all. "Thanks."

"Wireless password is posted on the chalkboard in the main room."

Wi-Fi. Well, at least there's that.

When I find the single cot tagged with the number 31, I shove my suitcase under the frame and then pull out my laptop and sit cross-legged on the thin mattress. I type in the wireless password and connect to the internet first, then hop over to my email inbox. Nothing is amiss, and while the donations from my website have slowed down, they're still coming in at a steady trickle every day.

I also see an appointment reminder for tomorrow from Kelly Fraser, LLP.

I hit reply on the email and explain quickly that I've left Chicago and won't be home for a while. I request to cancel the appointment and then hit send on the email.

I spend a little time looking at local jobs on the internet, but I keep coming back to the fact that my most lucrative skill is being a hype girl for people online. Pivoting the Mia Starr brand into life coaching or something else would have been an option, but it isn't now that Jesika's face is all over my feed impersonating me.

I wish then that I would have had the cab driver stop by a

wireless store so I could buy a new SIM card for my phone. While most hotels and businesses in the area don't take alternate forms of digital payment, I think an electronics store will. Paying digitally has the added benefit of not allowing anyone to track me in the event that my bank account statements are subpoenaed, just in case Dean's attack comes back to bite me.

A notification dings a moment later, alerting me to a new email. My therapist has replied and offered to reschedule my appointment to a more convenient time. I type out a quick reply and explain that I'm currently stuck in Tahoe without hotel accommodation until I get a new credit card in the mail.

She replies to that email quickly with a surprising offer.

Tahoe. I spent a lot of winter vacations there in college. Haven't been in a long time. What do you say we do your next session in person?

My heart drops when I realize she means she can come here —to see me.

I respond to her email, *okay,* and then leave it at that. Let her come. It doesn't mean I have to meet with her. I can ghost her when she gets here if I'm not feeling up to it. But the truth is...Kelly Fraser has become a bit of a safe space for me through the chaos. I find that I kind of *want* to see her.

Perfect. I'll email when I land and let you know where I'm staying.

I don't reply.

"You doin' work or somethin'?" Vocal cords that sound like they've been ravaged by decades of cigarette use shock me.

"Just looking for work," I reply, careful to close any tabs that show personal information.

The woman hangs over my shoulder. "No work 'round here 'less you know how to cater to the rich folk."

I nod, practically choking on the smell of cigarettes that follows her like her own personal aura.

"You from here?"

"No," I answer, already sick of this line of questioning. "I've had a rough day. Think I'm gonna go to sleep now." I close my laptop and tuck it against my chest, spooning it in the fetal position on the lumpy cot. The slow throb that's been pressing at my skull escalates to a freight train as my vision begins to waver and blur.

"Friendly much? Geez, you city folk are all the same."

"Whatever," I whisper.

"Come again?" My neighbor leans closer.

"Name's Maya," I spit. "Nice to meet you."

"There are those manners. I'm Gertie. Nice to meet you, *city girl*."

Chapter Thirty-Five

"You look great." Kelly waits for me to stand from my chair in the Drip Drop. When I don't, she bends and offers me an awkward hug. She sticks out like a sore thumb in this place. Her old Louis Vuitton tote bag is coming apart at the seams, and the vibrant red fur collar that's wrapped around her neck is more Vegas showgirl than Tahoe ski bunny.

Despite my aversion to her outdated style, I offer a smile and a quick hug.

"You look wonderful. Did you have a good flight?" I say the thing one is supposed to say in this moment.

"Oh, it was great. I loved seeing the mountains when we came in. What brought you to Tahoe?"

"I was going to head home to LA, but then I saw the direct flight to Tahoe and I thought a little detour to the mountains might be fun."

"I guess so. I love how spontaneous you are lately." Her smile is warm, her eyes holding mine as she sits and unfurls the red fur from her neck. I flash back to Dean's lifeless eyes as I choked him with my gasoline-soaked scarf, and then I instantly push the thought from my skull. The dark daydreams have been plaguing me more than usual lately, so much so that I've been toying with the idea of asking Kelly if she thinks I should be on some sort of medication.

"I'm trying to master the art of self-care," I offer cheerfully.

"Well, that can't be easy. You've been through so much the last few weeks." Kelly points to the counter. "Did you order? Can I get you something?"

"No, I've had enough coffee today."

"Okay, give me a minute." She stands and moves to the counter to order.

She's so nice, I wonder what she sees in me.

"So, tell me all about Chicago. Did you enjoy yourself?" She's back, folding her scarf in her lap and using it like a blanket to offer her some warmth. We're both LA girls and so out of our element in the cold mountain climate.

"Chicago was okay. City life isn't for me. I like the energy, but all the concrete just gets to feeling oppressive. I'm loving the fresh mountain air."

"I bet, such a change of scenery. And the men all have beards and mountain boots. It's so sexy."

"Oh, lookin' for a hot date, are we?" I'm teasing her, and it's starting to feel a little more like a friendship.

"If the opportunity presents itself." She shrugs flirtatiously, and it makes me giggle. "We should grab dinner and a drink tonight. Have you been anywhere nice?"

"No, I haven't had the time. Or the budget. I'm waiting on my new credit card to arrive."

"Oh, that's right. Where have you been staying?"

"I tried the backpacker's hostel," I start with. "But they only take credit cards for payment."

"Oh." She sips her coffee and listens carefully.

"So, the women's shelter was my only option. I told them my husband was abusive. I'm not wrong."

"No. No, you're not." She seems to be choosing her words wisely.

"My new card should arrive tomorrow."

"Well, if it doesn't, I'm happy to help however I can. I've only booked my hotel through Sunday, but if you need, I could call and ask for a room with an extra bed or a cot at least."

"No, that's kind of you, but there's not much difference between a cot at the shelter and a cot in a fancy hotel room. I'm asleep, so I don't even know the difference."

"Yes, but still..." She takes another sip of her coffee. "I hate to think of you sleeping in a room with a bunch of strangers."

"It's safe," I whisper. "Mostly."

"Mostly?" she inquires.

"There's just this one lady...Gertie. She's so intimidating, I end up sleeping with my laptop and phone under my pillow just so she doesn't steal them. And speaking of my phone, I haven't even been using it much since our last session."

"Oh?" She curls her palms around her cup and leans in.

"I've just been thinking how little it brings to my life. So I haven't been on social media in two days. I've been using my time at the shelter to really pause and reflect."

"This all sounds wonderful." She finishes her coffee and then slides it to the edge of the table. "What do you say we go visit where you've been staying?"

"Why?" I can't suppress the cringe, just thinking of going back there so soon.

"I just want to make sure you're safe. And I wouldn't mind going for a drive. I have this rental car. I might as well use it."

"Okay," I say, packing up my things and then pushing my arms through my coat.

A few minutes later, we're heading south on Highway 50. The small shelter I'm staying at is only a few miles out of the main village. We'll be there in less than five minutes, and yet every moment feels like torture. I'm not used to letting people get so close—and worse, I haven't even fully decided what I should tell her and what I should keep to myself.

The rest of the ride is silent until I point her into the parking lot of the women's services building. I'm suddenly embarrassed, but then, what does this woman mean to me? She can't affect my brand, and she doesn't know Dean or Jesika. She hardly knows about Mia—I've mentioned little about my online persona to her, but I don't doubt that if she wanted to, she could find me with a few quick internet searches.

"My! You're back early. Wanna help with slop duty in the kitchen tonight?" Gertie is lingering near the sidewalk, smoking a cigarette, when we pull into a parking spot.

Kelly looks cautious and reserved. She's probably regretting that she offered to bring me here. "I think you should stay with me. Your credit card will be here tomorrow. It's no big deal."

My mind whirs as another headache builds. Her offer, without a doubt, violates some sort of patient-therapist agreement, but I'd say yes to just about anyone so I don't have to spend another night in the shelter.

"Are you sure?" I breathe.

"I think it's for the best, dear." Kelly wraps an arm around my shoulder and pulls me to her in a quick hug. "I won't even charge you for the overtime counseling sessions."

We both laugh, and it's then I think that this woman might be my chance. With her help, I can gather support and resources and make the best decision for my future. She is my lifeline.

"Thank you. Your generosity means more than words can even say."

"Great. Let's pack you up and get you out of here."

I smile sweetly, thankful for the generosity of this woman. Her friendship has been a blessing, and I sense that she will be integral to securing my freedom and giving me another chance at life.

Kelly and I are connected now, whether she knows it or not.

Chapter Thirty-Six

"I'm thinking of volunteering at the shelter."

"Volunteering?" Kelly is holding a glass of red wine in one hand as she gazes out over the cityscape later that evening. We're having after-dinner drinks at the rooftop lounge of her hotel. Gas fireplaces are glowing shades of orange around the roof, and cozy sofas decorated with knit blankets and Western-style throw pillows anchor the fires. The lounge is busy with people dripping in real furs, winter boots, and expensive ski attire.

"I've been thinking I could stay here awhile."

"Stay? In Tahoe?" She finishes her glass of wine and then gestures to the waitstaff for a refill.

"I like it. I like the energy and the people. There are plenty enough coffee shops for me to work in."

"But what about your place in LA?"

"I could rent it out, maybe."

"You think this is the place for you? I know you like the mountain air, I do too, but it's so far removed from anything worth doing…"

I sip my wine slowly, enjoying the taste of the California

grapes on my taste buds. Kelly and I spent most of the day together, and hotel management was able to move her to a room with two beds. I promised to reimburse her when I'm able, but she insisted that the price is the same whether I'm there or not. She's very kind. I wonder if she's always so open with everyone she meets or if she feels a special connection with me because we've been talking weekly for almost two decades.

"I think you shouldn't rush to make any life decisions. Just enjoy the mountain air and relax. You've been through a lot lately."

"I have." I sip my wine again. I wonder how she knows that. I've only told her that Dean has left me. She doesn't know a thing about anything else. Or does she? The hairs on the back of my neck rise as I wonder exactly what her motives are for coming all the way out here. "Maybe I could find a temporary rental."

"Hmm." Her eyes are trained on the yellow streetlamps that peek through the snow-laden evergreens surrounding the hotel. It feels like we have a bird's-eye view of the village from here, and while we can't see the ski slopes through the trees, I know they're lit up in the distance, the ski lifts carrying adventure-seekers to the mountaintop. I yearn for the easy life the people who come here have.

"You don't think I should stay?"

Her eyes scan the crowd and then land on me again. "Well, I just don't see why you'd want to."

"I could take up skiing. Or be a nanny for the wealthy families who visit."

"You...want to take care of kids?"

I shrug. "I could."

"But do you want to?"

"Maybe."

"It just doesn't seem like a *you* kind of thing to do."

"Well, what does?"

She doesn't answer. The truth is, I've always felt like this—a bit of a lost soul wandering and wondering which way the wind will blow me next.

"It's just…" I ponder how much to share with this woman. "I've been so attached to my online brand…unplugging and taking it easy for a while sounds refreshing."

"For a weekend, maybe," she quips. She must be at least a little drunk, and I think how funny it is that Kelly Fraser is the kind of person that gets drunk with a stranger on their first night together. I don't think I've ever trusted anyone as much as she's trusting me right now.

"So, how's your sister doing?"

One of Kelly's Botoxed brows twitches. "She's mad at me right now."

"Oh?"

"Says I should have been there for her more during her move. I just couldn't rearrange my schedule to help her like she expected, I guess." Her words are a little slurred.

"That's too bad. When's the last time you talked to her?" I want to keep her talking about something other than me.

"Oh, not since she left my apartment a few weeks ago. She does this sometimes. She'll go a year and not talk to me and then come back into town like nothing happened. It's pretty annoying, but I realize she's working through her own life stuff. It's just hard because she's the only family I have left, and she hardly seems to care most of the time."

"That's too bad." I hum empathetically. "I always wanted a sister. It sounds like I didn't miss out on much, though."

"Oh, I love her. We love each other, we just can't live with each other. Even as kids, we fought and fought." She pushes a hand through her wavy blond hair. "We have a lot of good memories too, though."

207

"Families are so complicated," I offer. "That's why I was thinking volunteering at the shelter—working with women in need—maybe it would fill something inside me that's been empty." I look around the rooftop, so many well-dressed men and women chatting and drinking and eating. "I have so much access, I could help advocate on their behalf. And they would be helping me as much as I'm helping them. Spending time at the shelter and hearing some of their stories..." I pause for effect. "I realize I've been living such an emotionally unhealthy lifestyle. So much of my self-worth has been plugged into my brand, into what strangers think of me on the internet. It feels like I've been living a fake life and I want to stop, but I don't know how."

A long pause lingers between us as the waiter pours more wine into both of our glasses. When he's gone, I begin to wonder exactly what he's overheard. I feel on edge, like I can't trust anyone. And I think it's because Tahoe is so far removed from the rest of the world that I like it.

"Talking to those women gives me hope that I can get back to normal again. If I can vow to stay off social media—take a long hiatus—it will be good for me, and I think I have a chance at succeeding here. If I go back to LA, I'm just going to backslide into depression and ruminating over what went wrong with us."

"Us?" She hums like she's forgotten who I'm speaking about. What the hell are all of those notes for if she's not going to remember the specifics of my situation?

"Dean and me."

"You still think of him?"

"Yes."

"Often?"

"Yes."

"And you still think of the two of you as an *us*?"

"I'm afraid I always will," I confess.

"A divorce is likely one of the hardest things you'll endure," she muses.

"I'm still bitter about what he did and how he handled things."

"I know." She lets my thoughts linger. "But he's moved on, hasn't he? I think the more you can train your brain away from thoughts of Dean and focus on the things you can control—"

"I can't control anything. I feel powerless. I just want to... I don't know. I just want to...make it all go away."

She nods, holding her wineglass in one hand and watching me with curious intent. "I think it's important that you live in reality, Shae. Try to take each moment as it comes and not live in your mind so much. Some people lose themselves when they spend too much time thinking and not enough time living."

"I know," I spit. "That's why I'm throwing away my phone. Or at least thinking about it. I realize now that the world I created virtually is impacting my reality in ways I didn't antici-pate. It's like I'm manifesting—ah...never mind. I'm ready to close the book on this stage of my life, is all I'm saying. I'm ready to shut down the Mia Starr brand."

Shit. I know I've made a mistake as soon as the words are out of my mouth. I've been careful to avoid using the name of my online persona. I assess her reaction, trying to determine whether she's picked up on my slip of the tongue.

"That sounds like a good idea," is all she says.

"I may never own another phone. And I'll never touch social media again. I really feel like I've turned a page. Leaving Chicago was the best thing for me."

"Social media isn't a bad thing when it's managed the right way."

I let her words sink in, still trying to figure out if she's here as a friend, therapist, or as something else entirely.

"I just don't think it's a smart move for me. I'm afraid if I went back to social media, I might be tempted to…" I can't exactly tell her I would be tempted to take on a new identity. Living someone else's life, at least for a little while, is so alluring. Who knows what bad things could happen next time? So I'm committed to making sure there is no next time.

"Tempted to what?" Kelly probes.

"Tempted to let it take over my life again," is all I say. I'm suddenly uncomfortable with her here. I'm sure I've revealed too much. "I think this wine has gone to my head. I should probably turn in for the night."

"Okay. I think I'll finish my glass before heading down. Do you want my keycard?"

"Sure."

She fishes in her bag and then passes me the room key.

"See ya in a bit?"

She nods. "Goodnight, Shae."

I walk back to the room, my thoughts whirring as I wonder how much I can trust this woman. She's been nothing but positive and supportive, but I'm still stuck on how much she really knows about what I've done. How much does she even know me at all? Every time she calls me Shae, I shudder—I don't feel like that person anymore. I'm ready to put Shae to bed. Mia Starr is my future.

By the time I reach the hotel room, tears have sprung to my eyes as I think about missing Dean. He wasn't a perfect man, but he was mine. He still is mine. I just can't let go when he's been the center of my existence for so long.

Living without Dean feels like living with a phantom limb.

Chapter Thirty-Seven

"**G**ood morning." Kelly wipes the sleep from her eyes before she crawls out of bed Saturday.

"Morning," I murmur, my thoughts dialed into the laptop screen in front of me. I've been up for hours, while she's been snoring off her wine hangover.

"Whatcha working on?" Kelly asks when she returns from the bathroom a minute later. I minimize the tabs I have open—I've been searching for any news about Bishop in Chicago, but I haven't found a word. Some dark side of me wants to text him, but I know that won't lead anywhere good. I'm dying to know what happened after the meetup in Millennium Park, but I can't risk reaching out.

"Who's that?"

The question pulls me out of my thoughts. I'd almost forgotten she was here. "Huh?"

"Your wallpaper—who is that?"

I glance at my screen and realize, with all the tabs minimized, Kelly can now see my wallpaper. It's the most recent photo from Jesika's newsfeed—a photo of her and Dean. His face is in shadow and you can really only make out some of his features, but I can tell it's him. Jesika has her arms wrapped around him, and she's puckered up to plant a kiss on his stubbled cheek. It's hard to make out much of Jesika's face because she's shrouded in waves of silvery hair. But if I squint, I find it's easy to pretend it's Dean and me. It's giving me comfort right now while we're apart. A part of me still hopes this is temporary, that he'll get sick of catering to Jesika's every whim and come back to me.

"Oh, that's my sister and her fiancé," I finally reply, pressing my fingertips to my temples with a frown.

"Oh." Confusion ripples her features. "I didn't know you had a sister." *I don't.* "She looks like you." She smiles. "She's very pretty."

"She's gorgeous." I hope Kelly can't hear the bitterness that laces my voice. "And ridiculously high-maintenance. I feel bad for her fiancé."

"More power to her." Kelly winks and then heads to the other side of her bed to look for something in her luggage. "Wait, I thought you said you always wanted a sister when I was talking about mine?"

"Stepsister, she's a stepsister." I bite out.

"Oh." She continues to dig through her bag. "I'm so glad the hotel could move us to a bigger room. Did you sleep well?"

"I did," I answer. I'm not used to having anyone to answer to, and annoyance at all her chatty questions is weighing on me. I'd rather be left alone. I think I'd almost prefer the women's shelter to Kelly right now. "I've already called the hotel. They said the mail is usually delivered around noon. I'm going to plan to be there." I work my fingertips back and forth across my forehead with a wince, willing the throbbing to subside.

"Do you have a migraine?"

"I've been getting them more here," I confirm.

"It's altitude sickness, poor thing." She frowns. "Let me help." She crosses the room to me and before I can protest her fingers are working at the base of my neck and spine. She hums softly and then admits, "My mother always had migraines. My sister and I used to take turns rubbing her head and telling her about our school days. Those are some of my favorite memories with her." She works back and forth silently and then moves to my temples and continues her massage.

I can't help when a small sigh escapes my lips. Not even Dean was ever this tender and giving, and while Kelly's massage feels nice, it also makes me uncomfortable on a deep level.

"There, doesn't that feel good?" Kelly moves to my side to look me in the eye. "A little Motrin and a lot of water should help." Kelly's eyes linger on mine. My skin begins to feel tight and itchy under her gaze. Like I'm wearing a mask and she's just about to uncover my real identity. "You're so beautiful, Shae." She smiles sweetly. "Such beautiful skin and wide, expressive eyes. If we had a little more time here, I'd say we should have a spa day and get facials and everything." Her eyes gleam with the wholesome possibility of it. My stomach twists with aversion.

I don't have a reply because the cold truth is that if we were in Los Angeles right now, we wouldn't be friends. I would rather be dead than get caught with her and her ratchet Louis bag in Beverly Hills.

"I should get ready to leave." I stand abruptly.

"Oh sure, let me get dressed and we can head out. Maybe we can grab coffee and some breakfast first." She rushes to grab the nearest clothes folded neatly in her suitcase.

"Oh, no worries. You've been so kind already. I'll just call the cab driver who left me his business card. I'm sure he'd be happy to bring me up there to get my credit card."

"Oh no, don't be silly. It's no big deal at all. I'd love to drive you up there. I bet it's a gorgeous drive." She seems committed.

I sigh. "Okay. If you're sure…"

"Oh yes, definitely."

Thirty minutes later, Kelly and I are headed north. The two-lane road winds through throngs of snowcapped evergreens as the mountains loom in the distance. My nerves are on edge, I'm not sure what the next step is if my card doesn't arrive today, but I've decided I can't think about that until I have to. Jesika hasn't posted on social media since our night on the Riverwalk, and it's got my brain buzzing with the reasons why. Maybe she's sick or not feeling well again. I've flirted with the idea that the worst has happened, but after searching news articles and police reports from that night and the next, I've come up empty-handed. Because of this, I've started to assume she's fine, has made a full recovery from her fall, and that she and Dean are probably on the mend right now. I have to think that, because the alternative is far darker than I'm willing to handle. My memory is hazy of that night, but I know that anything that unfolded was an accident—pure and simple.

I've even started to tell myself that soon enough, Dean will realize that staying with Jesika is hazardous—they're not meant to be. He and I are connected in ways I never knew possible. We're forged in fire, and our bonds can't be severed so easily.

"Well, isn't this fancy." Kelly's words pull me from my thoughts. "I should have booked here."

Her rental car is pulling into the cobblestone drive of the sprawling mountain lodge. Flagstone and hand-hewn logs anchor the oversized entryway. A valet pushes through the doors and bows quickly as we pull to a stop.

"Is the restaurant open for brunch?" she asks him through the window.

"It is, ma'am."

"Perfect. I'll let you park the car, and we'll go grab some brunch while we wait for your mail to arrive."

"Okay." I'm hardly paying attention to her words, my heart is pounding so loudly in my ears.

Kelly hands the valet her keys, and he passes her a pink valet ticket. She tucks it into her ragged Louis bag and then gestures for me to enter the hotel.

"Excuse me," I breathe as soon as I see the concierge. "Do you know if the mail has been delivered?"

"Yes, I believe it has, ma'am."

"Perfect."

"Should be behind the check-in desk." He nods to the woman in the matching blue-collared uniform behind a mahogany desk.

"Thank you." I cross the lobby and greet her kindly before asking if the mail has arrived for the day. She nods and smiles, patting the stack of mail next to her. "Do you have something addressed to Shae Halston?"

The woman takes a long moment to unwrap the rubber band from the handful of white envelopes. She reads the address of each one carefully, putting one envelope on the desk beside her as she moves to the next. Soon, she reaches the end and then turns to me with a frown.

"I'm sorry. Nothing here for that name." She smiles, and it raises the hair on the back of my neck.

"Can you check again, please?"

Her eyes darken, and then she catches herself and forces the cheerful grin again. "Of course."

She holds the stack again, moving through each one slowly until I get so agitated I snatch the remaining envelopes from her hand and spread them out on the desk in front of me.

"Miss!" She moves to snatch them back, but I block her, using my arms to cover the various white envelopes. I refuse to give her back a single one until I've seen them all for myself. "Miss, don't make me call security."

"This is very important. Please," I plead, passing her back an envelope that I've confirmed isn't addressed to me. *It has to be here.* "I can't believe it's not here."

"I have to ask you to please leave, before I call—"

"I'm leaving." I wave her off, already backing away.

"Shae?" Kelly is watching me, head cocked to the side. *Shit.* She's just seen everything unfold. *Double shit.* I definitely look unhinged. But wouldn't anyone after being denied access to all their money? Dean managed to lock down every credit card in both of our names, and I was the fool who failed to ever establish credit on my own with a separate account and card. Everything we have is shared.

"I don't know what to do," I sob, covering my face in my hands and bursting into tears.

Kelly comes closer, wrapping me in her arms and stroking my back. "We'll figure it out, honey. I promise."

"I guess I have to go back to women's services. If they have a bed."

"No, no—you're gonna stay with me one more night. We have plenty of time to figure out your next move. Your card will probably arrive by Monday anyway—or maybe we could call your bank and explain what happened and they could send you a wire to one of the banks here?"

I take a deep breath, forcing myself to calm down. "Maybe."

"My flight leaves around noon tomorrow. I could call and ask for a late checkout for the room—that will give you a few more hours to figure this out too."

"You're so sweet, the best friend I've ever had." I try to blink away what feels like a stabbing blade in my skull.

Her eyes bleed concern as she rubs both of my shoulders

with her palms. "Tomorrow is a new day. I bet we can even get you back to LA if we put our minds to it."

I sniff. She passes me a tissue from her purse. "Thank you for being here for me. I've been a mess lately."

"That's okay, honey. I'm always here for you. Remember that—you're never alone. I'm only ever a phone call away. We're practically like sisters."

Chapter Thirty-Eight

"Should I charge it to your room, ma'am?" The barista behind the bar at the hotel hands me a steaming hot latte.

"Yes. Can you charge it to my room—number 1001, last name Fraser."

"Yes, miss."

I back away from the counter, feeling a little on edge as I take my first sip of coffee. I thought Tahoe was a good fit for me, but now I'm not so sure. I told Kelly I needed caffeine ASAP this morning and that I'd meet her in the lobby since I'd finished packing before her.

My mind crawls through a thousand terrible possibilities as fevered anxiety floods my system. I haven't even been gone from LA for a month, and no matter how hard I try to outrun my problems, they keep catching up to me. Out of the corner of my eye, I register that the elevator doors have just slid open, and Kelly is standing there, luggage in one hand, ragged Louis bag in the other.

She's been a good friend the last few days, but still, I don't trust her.

My muscles begin to tremble and shake as the hot latte splashes over the lip of my to-go cup and scalds my hand. I drop the coffee, and the hot liquid bleeds into the elegant Oriental rug.

"Shae?" Kelly calls, but I can't move my lips to answer her. Tears flood my eyes as I realize what's probably happened. Why I haven't heard from Dean or Jesika or even Bishop. Why Jesika's social media has been silent. And I bet Kelly coming here isn't even as straightforward as I wanted to believe.

"Shae?" Kelly bends, placing a concerned hand on my shoulder.

"Get away from me," I seethe. I can't think; I can only feel, and right now, everyone feels like the enemy. "Who sent you?"

"Excuse me?" Confusion wrinkles her brow.

"Answer me. Who sent you?"

"No one. No one sent me, Shae. I came to see you and get some fresh mountain air—"

"No. No. No, you didn't." I turn, aiming for the front doors. I haven't even reached the all-glass revolving doors when it hits me. "You were wired, weren't you?"

"What? No, of course not. I'm not allowed—"

"Liar," I spit just as the first flash of red reflects in the glass doors.

"Shae—"

"Shae Halston? You're under arrest for the assault and attempted murder of Jesika Layman and Dean Halston. Anything you say—"

"No, that's not me! You have the wrong person! My name is Mia Starr!"

Chapter Thirty-Nine

Kelly Fraser, LLP

ne Year Later

"Do you want to see my husband? He's very handsome." Shae's eyes sparkle as she passes me the small, framed photo she's been cupping to her chest.

I turn it over, smile sweetly at a photo of Dean and Jesika together, and then pass it back to her. "You make a beautiful couple."

"We're expecting a baby." Shae rubs her rounded belly.

"Oh, really?" I pretend to be surprised. This is what she says every week. All our visits are the same, and still, I keep coming. "Do you know what the date is?"

Shae doesn't respond. She's not the woman who sauntered into my office as a teenager twenty years ago, that's for sure. I suppose that's why I'm here. To try to uncover what happened—where things went wrong—and if I could have done something different. Maybe I didn't push her enough, or maybe by the time I found her at the tender age of seventeen her destructive patterns were already set.

Of all my cases, hers haunts me the most.

"Mia honey, time to take your meds." Shae's head snaps up

as she glares at the nurse who's just come into the room. "That's a girl," the nurse purrs as Shae swallows down the pill she's been passed.

"Any progress with Shae?" I ask the nurse, just as I do every week.

She gives a curt shake of her head and then leaves the room.

Shae was sentenced three months ago to Pacific View Adult Psychiatric Hospital. Thankfully, the judge allowed me to continue to visit her while she withered away in a jail cell awaiting her trial. The reality of Shae's situation was far worse than even she could have realized. In truth, Bishop had flipped on her to gain favor with the judge, and he, in turn, froze all of her assets before she'd even left Chicago.

"My husband is visiting me this weekend. He works so hard. I'm so lucky. He's practically a workaholic." Shae—or Mia, as she prefers to be called—traces her fingertip along Dean's smiling face. "He's so determined to support our family. I just know he'll be the best dad." She's rubbing her belly again. She did this throughout the trial—according to Shae, she's been expecting Dean's baby for over a year now. While I admit she has gained some weight, she hardly looks pregnant. The internet sleuths were up in arms when Shae was sentenced. Many claimed her insanity plea was all an act, right down to her claims of being pregnant with her husband's baby.

"How do the new medications make you feel?" I avoid using her name at all. I've been trying to work with her to come back to Shae's reality, but so far, she only responds to being called Mia.

"I hate the meds." Anger distorts her face. "I wish I didn't have to take them."

"Do they make your mind feel foggy? That's what you complained about with the last medication."

"They all make me feel foggy. Why don't you try taking

them?" Shae looks up at me, and for a moment, I swear I see a flicker of awareness in her strained expression. She's not quite the girl that I knew, and I wonder if she ever will be again. I suppose this is why I still visit her, because no one else will. I am her only family, and during the trial, it was just me and her legal and medical team behind her in the courtroom. The prosecution, on the other hand, was overflowing with Dean and Jesika's network of friends and fans, and the judge had to limit the number of news media allowed into the courtroom due to fire code capacity restrictions.

Shae's trial was standing room only. She made history, so much so that before the final arguments were given, she was already turning down deals from all the major streaming platforms to tell her story. Shae was famous, and one of the biggest internet true crime forums dubbed her *The Widow Influencer*. Internet headlines were taken with her girl-next-door beauty and her brash sense of audacity to commit fraud to the tune of over $100,000. *Page Six* coined her the internet's biggest grifter, and the wild part was that through all of it, she found her supporters. Some women's groups defended her actions by stating she was only doing what she could within a unbalanced, patriarchal system. Shae did what she had to in a man's world; she was merely a pawn at the whim of privileged and entitled men like Dean.

Each day of her trial was live streamed, and some true crime forums even had watch parties as they waited for her sentence to be read. Shae was a true crime sensation in the era of feminism and gender politics, and everyone had a different opinion. A women's rights lawyer even wrote an op-ed for the Sunday edition of *The New York Times*, explaining that the very act of putting a mentally ill woman on trial and televising it was a sexist move perpetrated by a profoundly flawed capitalist society, and that every woman, and every man who loves women, should petition for Shae's release. Where was the justice in a young, single woman being victimized by a male-dominated system, one that overlooks mental health in favor of punishing the mentally ill for crimes their illness led them to commit? Mental health advocates decried the lack of solid support within the justice system for women dealing with severe mental illnesses, and that a broken healthcare system was to blame for the ongoing struggles Shae faced as she spiraled and continued to lose her sanity.

And the cameras loved her. Shae seemed to play into her misunderstood It girl role. She came to the courthouse with her hair in elegant chignons or soft waves, and she wore tailored designer suits or demure cashmere sweaters and pencil skirts by upscale labels. Fashion blogs popped up following each of her daily courtroom style choices, and the hashtag *#TeamMia* was flooded with outfit inspirations after each appearance. The internet buzzed with which stylist she used, because surely she couldn't be making her own fashion choices when she was so clearly mentally unstable in every other aspect.

Ironically, if Shae were ever to be released from her sentence, she would have endless opportunities awaiting her. Oprah herself would jump at the chance to talk to her, but right now...right now, Shae doesn't even know her own name.

I have faith that someday she'll walk out of this hospital. Maybe with the right mix of medications and therapy, she can come back from the brink and live a healthy and productive life. Her determination and creativity and sense of imagination are unmatched. She could go far if only she could keep two feet grounded in reality.

Some days, I see glimmers of calm rationality. But for the most part, I'm forced to speak to Mia about her marriage to Dean and their unplanned but very welcome surprise pregnancy. Our sessions seem frozen in time, and still, I hesitate to push her delicate psyche too far—she's been through so much. It feels like I am the last person to have really been with *Shae*. After her arrest by federal agents in the hotel lobby in Lake Tahoe, Shae vanished. The next time I was able to see her—weeks later, after her transfer back to LA County—Shae was gone, and in her place was a manic and deranged Mia. She babbled incoherently and cried uncontrollably. I have no doubt that the way her case was mishandled between the time of her arrest and my first meeting with her in jail is responsible for the shell of a woman that exists before me today.

Had Shae been prescribed the medications she needed from the beginning, she might still be with me.

"Do you remember Bishop?"

She blinks, then her expression hardens and she shakes her head.

"You and he had a brief relationship while you were in Chicago." Not a single twinge of recognition crosses her face, so I continue. "He was arrested in Millennium Park for the assault of your husband—do you remember that?" She shakes her head nearly imperceptibly. "He also stole your diamond ring." Still nothing. "He had it with him that night." I watch her in search of any flicker of remembrance. "Do you remember the canary diamond Dean gave you?"

"Where is it?" comes her expressionless inquiry.

"It was decided it would be best to pawn it to fund your defense."

"That's a one-hundred-thousand-dollar ring."

"And you had a one-hundred-thousand-dollar legal team. You were found not guilty by way of insanity—I think it was worth it."

"Speak for yourself," she mumbles and then drops her eyes back to the floor. The light has dimmed in her eyes, and her lips form a thin, tight line, almost as if she's zipped them shut.

"What about the money from the donations?"

"The ones you took under the guise of paying for your husband's funeral? A few people have gotten together to bring a civil case to court, but there isn't any money left. And...well, I guess not signing those divorce papers didn't work in your favor. If you had, the judge would have granted you alimony or forced Dean to liquidate all the real estate to give you what you deserve, but...well, there just isn't anything left."

She doesn't respond, and I spend a few more moments watching Shae gaze at the small, framed photo. I realize then how much I've given up for this woman, only to watch her destroy herself. I crossed boundaries somewhere along the way, but I did it with the purest intentions—because I thought if Shae only had a friend to confide in, maybe it would be enough. The trial and surrounding media storm took its toll, and I'm afraid I still haven't recovered. I recognize that, at some point, I'll need to close the case file on Shae and move on, but I'm not sure I know who I am or what I want if I don't have this case to spin my wheels over at night with a bottle of wine. I've stuck my neck out for Shae, and she doesn't even realize it.

I walk down the long hallway of the hospital, stopping at the nurses desk to check out and offer a friendly wave to the nurse before I exit the building and walk to the parking lot. I've been thinking about moving my practice up the coast. My brief time with Shae in Tahoe brought back a lot of memories, and I admit I've been yearning for the sense of peace the Northern California woods can offer. I've even gone so far as to reach out to a real estate agent in the area and inquire about rentals that have an office for my practice. I mentioned the move to my sister the last time we spoke—she's off hiking Tibet before spending the winter at an ashram in India. With everyone else going through significant life changes, I find myself feeling a little left out.

Just left Shae. She's still disassociated. The new

meds don't seem to make a difference. I send the first message and then send another in quick succession. **Now may be a good time for you to visit. It might be just the dose of reality she needs.**

I slide behind the wheel of my car and wait for a response. There are many things Shae doesn't understand about her time in Chicago, and yet one thing she does: her husband is still alive.

Dean and Shae aren't even technically divorced. Before she could sign the papers, Jesika was bleeding out on the Chicago Riverwalk, and Dean was fighting for his life on a ventilator. Jesika never recovered, and after some time on life support, her parents chose to let her pass in peace. Dean was distraught. I know because I've been talking to him nearly every week since the trial ended.

Shae's defense team tried to explain her erratic and ultimately deadly behavior as a crime of passion. When Dean served her divorce papers, it caused her mental illness to manifest, and from that point on, she split from reality. The judge didn't buy it in the beginning, and Shae was forced to stand trial. But the more the judge and jury witnessed Shae's devolution, the more the answer became clear.

I'm not ready. Dean's reply finally comes, and I can't say I blame him.

I frown as I try to advocate for my patient. **I just think she could use the gentle reminder that you've moved on and that she can turn over a new leaf too...**

I think back on one of the countless missteps Shae made during her time in Chicago. After Bishop attacked Dean, police investigators recommended Dean install a security camera in the garage, and he did the very next week. Shae is on camera coming and going from Dean's house almost as frequently as if it were her own. While the fact that Jesika and Shae had a real friendship held up in court for a while, by the time the jury was shown security footage of the night Shae tried to suffocate Dean with a gasoline-soaked scarf, her fate seemed sealed. All sympathy was replaced by revulsion.

Thankfully for Dean, Jesika had already been found and identified by the wallet and phone in her bag. Officers were already on the way to her home to speak to next of kin when Dean was found near death in his Audi. He spent three weeks on a ventilator and nearly a week in a coma—by the time the trial began, he was just starting physical therapy to learn to walk again.

My heart throbs in my chest as I consider what this man has been through at the hands of my patient. I'm not asking him to forgive her, only to understand that Shae wasn't born this way... tragedy tarnished her at a young age.

Before I have a chance to think better of it, I press dial on Dean's number. The line picks up almost instantly, and the only greeting is a soft grunt.

"Dean—there's something you don't know about her. I don't expect it to change your mind, but maybe if you understood where she comes from—"

"I know more than I need to know about Shae—that's not even the name she was born with, didya know that? Nothing about her is real. Don't let her fool you."

"Shae was diagnosed with dissociative identity disorder by a team of psychiatrists at Johns Hopkins after her sister died in an accident when she was fourteen."

"So?"

"Shae hasn't been the same since then. You've never known the real her, *she* doesn't even know the real her. All that she knows is this blurred sense of reality. She has selective amnesia about certain events and pieces of information."

"Convenient. I know this argument worked on the jury, but

have you forgotten that I lived with her? I watched her intentionally detach herself from me and her emotions and...reality."

"I understand, trust me. I've been her therapist for a long time. I've seen her through the many versions of Shae. She's always lived in a fantasy world because her reality was shattered when her sister died—"

"She never mentioned a sister," Dean mutters.

"She doesn't...her mind has buried the memory too deep. Shae lost herself to her pain that day, and she never came back. Her parents drove her back and forth across the country, looking for the best treatments, and after spending time with Shae, they all came to the same conclusion—her personality is too resistant to treatment, her disease will never be healed, only managed." I think on all of the inconsistencies in Shae's story. In the last few months during our time together before her arrest, the inconsistencies in our sessions became so regular I knew she was detaching from her past—almost shedding it like snakeskin. I corrected her at first, but then realized it would do more harm than good to have me correcting her all the time. So I decided then to let her speak. Her story is her story and there's nothing I can say that could change that.

"The people who suffer the most are the ones around her." Dean interrupts my thoughts.

"Her loved ones," I confirm sadly.

Dean sucks in a breath, and for the first time, I hear a hint of pain in his words. "I loved her once, Kelly, I did. But loving her cost me too much of myself." His tone lowers an octave. "I know what everyone thought when they saw me with Jesika. She was young and beautiful, but it was so much more than that. She was simple, and after Shae...I needed simple and straightforward. She was a breath of fresh air after all the manic manipulation that Shae created. I—" His words catch; I've never heard him so tender and thoughtful, "I'm not saying I was abused, but what she did—well..." He chokes. "I had to leave to save myself. It was me or her."

I nod. "I've been with Shae for a long time—I watched her fall in love with you, Dean. I've never seen her so happy. I know you did what you could, and I had hope for a while that love could keep her tethered to reality, but Shae's condition has gone untreated for too long. I've been her therapist for almost two decades—she was still a teenager when we first met. I think of her like the daughter I never had..." I sniff softly, "I can't leave her alone. What happens when no one comes to visit her? Who are any of us without the people who love us—really? Without people in our lives to remind us of who we are and what we stand for and why we're important...well, without love we're nothing more than strangers bumping up against each other in the night...temporary soul connections that evaporate as quickly as they appear. Without love, we're all just ghosts."

Dean doesn't respond, but I can hear his breaths coming over the line. I imagine that maybe he's crying like I am. It's only he and I who remain in her life now, and he's already abdicated his role. And then, just like he can read my mind, the line goes dead.

I am all she has left.

Dean's last text comes a moment later.

She ruined my life and stole my future. She's a murderer, and I'll likely live the rest of my life on disability. Now I'm supposed to show up for her to help her heal and find herself again? No thanks. I hope she burns in hell.

My heart squeezes in my chest as I realize Dean is a lost cause as far as Shae is concerned, and he's well within his rights to feel that way. Shae is alone in this world, and just like me, she'll probably die alone. Hot tears track down my cheeks as a deep sense of loneliness settles over me.

As I pull out of my parking spot, I resolve to turn over my own new leaf and make the move I've been putting off. With only one life to live, I decide to stop wasting it helping other people find themselves while sacrificing my own happiness and healing.

Shae has taught me much, and I can't regret my time with her. She has taught me to live in the moment and make the most of each opportunity that arises, and for that, I am forever grateful.

Chapter Forty

"How was your visit, dear?" The nurse enters my room with a kind smile.

Kelly has just left. I always feel better after Kelly visits. Few people really listen to a crazy person, but I find that Kelly still does. She almost regards me like I'm still *me*. Like we're still friends. I miss her friendship—truly—but in reality, I know I only showed her the side of me I wanted her to see.

"It was nice." I hum more to myself than anyone else.

White shoes shuffle across graying linoleum as she approaches me. She pats my back softly, then replies, "That's wonderful, dear. She's such a good influence on you."

"I told her all about the baby." I cradle my round stomach, warm tingles fluttering behind my rib cage at the thought of carrying my husband's child. "I think I'll name my baby after her, if I have a girl, of course. My husband thinks it will be a girl. He'll make a great girl dad."

The nurse nods, lips pressed in a thin line. "And how are the new meds making you feel? Anything different?"

I shake my head, refusing to make eye contact.

"Okay. Maybe that's a good sign." She holds a small plastic

cup containing a pill in one palm and a glass of tepid faucet water in the other.

I wince. "Do I really have to take them three times a day?"

"If you want them to work, you do," she retorts, just like she always does.

I take the plastic cup from her and toss the small pill into my mouth like I'm taking a shot. She watches me with the focus of a hawk, then gestures for me to open my mouth so she can inspect it. The nurses have been instructed to be extra diligent in confirming that I swallow my pills after my first week here when they had to pump my stomach. It's also the reason why they've switched my medications—the medicine gave me all-day nausea and a pounding headache. I faked the nurses out for the first week and didn't take them, then took them all at once late on my first Friday night here and got so sick I was emergency evacuated to the nearest hospital.

I wasn't trying to kill myself—as much as the doctors thought I was—I just couldn't stand to stay at the psych hospital a moment longer. I needed an out. I thought spending time at a regular civilian hospital would at least give me some breathing room, maybe some ideas about my next move. But instead, I was under constant surveillance and lost more freedom than I gained.

I stayed in the hospital for four nights.

Upon my return to Pacific View Psychiatric, I was placed in the high-risk wing. Cameras were pointed at my small cot for the next thirty days. I was considered a security risk and forced to take every horse pill they brought me. But after a while, I settled in. I adapted to the routine of breakfast, group therapy, activity time, lunch, rest time, another activity, and then dinner. I began to look forward to group therapy. The social interaction left me feeling high off the buzz. I didn't know how much I'd missed people until I was forced to spend quality time with them every day. I also liked that spending time with them made me feel less fucked up.

I can't regret the knowledge I gained during my early time here. Because of my attempted overdose and subsequent trip to the hospital, I know the procedures in place to deal with an emergency situation, and I'm confident I can use what I've learned to make the next phase of my life work for me a little better than the current one.

"Do you need my help to get washed up for dinner, or will you be taking it in your room tonight?" The nurse, I've forgotten her name, is tidying my bathroom.

"I've got it tonight, thanks."

"You always seem so positive after she leaves." The nurse gazes at me with a thoughtful smile.

"Who? Kelly?" I say. "She's so kind. She says if I work with her long enough, I might be able to appeal my sentence with the judge and get time served, or even transferred to a lower-security facility."

"She said that?" Her thoughtful smile turns to a frown.

"Yes," I state.

"Well, it sounds like you've got your work cut out for you, then." She pats me on the shoulder. "I know you're just the girl to make it happen, too."

I nod. "It sounds like you've got your work cut out for you too."

"Yeah?" She's folding a hand towel now. "How so?"

"I heard the nurses talking about a nursing shortage and the strike the service workers are planning."

"You heard about that?" She seems surprised.

"During breakfast this morning. I was wrong to eavesdrop, but they *were* talking in the cafeteria in front of everyone."

"Well, I suppose you couldn't help it, then."

I nod, agreeing with her.

"It's going to be chaos tomorrow. They're planning a picket line, and I heard someone even tipped off the news media." The nurse turns away then, smiling softly as she retreats from my small room. "Let me know if you need anything."

I smile and wave as I watch her leave. "I've got everything I need now."

I shove my tongue around my mouth and eject the tiny white pill that was nestled in the uppermost corner. I spit it into my hand and, in a quick move, shove it into the tiny gap that exists between the cement block wall and the head of my single metal cot. Nurses are supposed to do a weekly sweep of the rooms of high-risk patients to check for hidden items, but because the nurses are so short-staffed, my room hasn't been searched since I moved in.

It's been more than six weeks since I've taken my medication at all, and I've never felt more clear.

Chapter Forty-One

Kelly Fraser, LLP

"Visitor for Room 22!"

"I can see myself to her room. I know you've got your hands full this morning." I reassure the nurse at check-in. It's only nine a.m., and already, she looks like she's been working the front lines. Something tells me she has, albeit picket lines.

"You sure?"

"I'm sure." I smile and start off down the narrow hallway. Nurses are speeding in and out of patient rooms as the general buzz of barely controlled chaos descends. I'd caught wind yesterday of a planned strike affecting healthcare and service workers, but I had no idea the kind of mayhem I was walking into this morning.

I hadn't planned on returning to visit Shae after our scheduled weekly appointment yesterday, but after spending all night planning the next phase of my life, I knew today would be my last chance to see her.

I'd already decided to honor my existing clients' appointments after my move. I was hopeful I could batch-schedule them during the week so I'd only to need to come to LA one or two days during the business week before they found a new therapist.

Not for Shae, though.

Shae has become an unhealthy obsession for me. I can't exactly pinpoint when I crossed the line, but it was well before I met with her in Tahoe.

Shae's regular nurse comes out of her room in a rush and nearly topples me.

"Oh! Excuse me. I was just coming to visit Shae."

"Oh, hi. I'm glad you're here." She pauses, looking genuinely relieved to see me. "She's been agitated all morning. Maybe you can calm her down."

"Agitated? She was fine when I left her yesterday."

"I don't know what happened." She frowns. "If you ask me, it's the crazy shit that's going on outside. It has all of my patients on edge this morning."

"Oh no." I'm not sure how many of their staff are striking today instead of working, but it's enough to have everyone flustered.

"She's reading a book in bed—hope it goes better for you than me." She nods to the door of Shae's room.

"Thanks," I murmur as the nurse hurries away.

As soon as I enter Shae's room, I know something is off. She's sitting silently in the corner, and it's as if she's in a daze. She's holding a book in her hands, all right, but I wouldn't say she's reading it.

"Shae?" I call, but she doesn't stir. I step closer. "Mia?"

Her eyes flicker and then settle on me. They shine bright, and I can't suppress my smile. I will miss my friend, even if we were never supposed to be friends to begin with. The hollow sense of loneliness that must permeate Shae's life doesn't sit well with me. I suppose it's the same sense of sadness I recognize in myself—when you have no family left and have never set down roots long enough to cultivate real and everlasting friendships. Through it all, Shae and I were there for each other. But not anymore.

"How are you feeling today, honey?" I bend to match her level. I pat her knee, encouraging her to open up to me.

Finally, she breathes. "I don't feel well. I feel like I'm getting sick. I feel like I haven't had fresh air in weeks—the asbestos in this ancient old building is killing me. It's probably killing my baby too."

"Shae, there's no asbestos."

"How do you know?" she spits out, and for the first time, I see her temper flare. "And don't call me that name. My name is Mia."

"Okay. Mia. I'm sorry about that. You said you're feeling sick. Would you like to go for a walk?"

Shae's eyes dart to the window. "They won't let me."

"Sure they will. I can ask."

Shae nods, closes her book, and then moves to stand at the window.

"How about you put your shoes on, and I'll go let them know we're going to take a little walk?"

Shae nods as I leave the room. I move down the hallway and pass a few more patient rooms before entering the main activity hall. The nurses station sits in the corner, and it's empty.

"Where is everyone?" I search for a nurse through the small groups of patients watching television and playing board games at tables.

"You need anything, dear? How's Shae? I told you she's off today, right?" Shae's nurse is passing through with a stack of patient files in hand.

"I think she's okay. Would it be okay if we went on a little walk? I think she just needs some fresh air."

The nurse glances around the room. "We're so short-staffed...she should really have approval from the on-call physician—"

"But I'm listed as primary medical personnel on her chart. Listen, I don't want to make your job worse today of all days, but she hasn't been outside in weeks. We'll be quick, I promise."

"Well, security is so tied up with what's going on outside, y'all could sneak out of the building and I couldn't do a thing about it."

"Well, we won't do that," I reassure her.

She nods, before a patient yells from down a long hallway, and she gives me a long-suffering look. "Enjoy your walk. I wish I were going with you."

I mouth a soft thank-you to her and then wave before heading back to Shae's room.

"Good news! We've been cleared for an adventure," I announce when I return.

What I find when I walk back into the room makes my heart sink. She's slumped in the chair, both shoes are on, but neither is tied. It looks as if she's just...forgotten what she was doing. I think now is probably not the time for me to tell Shae I will no longer be acting as her therapist. But then, there's never been a good time. Shae's life has been littered with drama and rock-bottom moments since I've known her. And while time heals most things, in Shae's case, it only dissolved what little sanity she had left. One of the court-appointed psychologists suggested schizophrenia as a logical explanation for Shae's splitting, but I think there's more to it. I just can't put my finger on what exactly.

Working quickly, I bend and tie her shoes and then swipe a cardigan that's thrown over the back of her chair.

"Ready, Shae? Let's go get some fresh air."

She doesn't respond. I wince when I realized I've used her old name again. I think about correcting myself or apologizing,

but I think better of it because at the end of the day, it's important that Shae live in reality. I think the nurses here are doing a
disservice calling her Mia, but then, I don't have to be her care-
giver every day.

And for the first time ever, it occurs to me that Shae may
never return. I've never allowed my mind to consider that possibility before. Giving up hope that I'll ever see my friend again
has never been an option, but maybe I've been living in my own
delusional reality. Maybe the reality is that Mia is here to stay
and Shae will only ever be a memory.

I hook my elbow in Shae's as we walk down the corridor.
Every step we take brings us closer to the heavy steel doors and
the small sliver of daylight that cuts through the double-paned
security window. One step closer to fresh air and freedom.

"It's beautiful outside today—not too hot, not too cold," I
offer as I swipe my keycard against the lockbox, and the door
buzzes open. The nurse's check-in station is empty, and I realize
how understaffed the hospital really must be today.

As soon as we're outside, Shae sucks in a breath of air. She
smiles as the sunshine lights up her cheeks, and she pats her
belly like she's sharing the sun's warmth with her unborn baby.
Shae has put on quite a lot of weight through her trial and
hospitalization; the stress coupled with the medications she's
been on have left a lasting mark. She looks as happy as I've seen
her since she arrived here, though, even if she does believe she's
pregnant with her ex-husband's baby. Shae has been operating
under this delusion for too long. If the state thinks that hospi-
tals like this one are rehabilitating patients, they couldn't be
more wrong. My time here with Shae has been proof enough of
that.

"Feels good, doesn't it, Shae?" I go out of my way to use her
real name again. She doesn't respond but continues to walk
slowly beside me. I guide her away from the groups of protestors

and walk in the opposite direction of the parking lot. "The grounds are so pretty, lots of flowers are in bloom right now."

"There's a vegetable garden in the back corner that they let some patients work on. I've asked them if I can work on it, but I haven't been approved yet."

"Oh. Well, that will be nice."

We walk for a while longer in silence. Once we're far enough away from the parking lot, the gentle buzz of people dies down, and it's just Shae and me and the towering evergreens that dot the manicured landscape. The path is littered with wild flowers and moss and beds of clover, and for a moment, I think it wouldn't be half bad to live here. It would be peaceful, to say the least, strikes and protestors aside.

"I heard a few of the patients talking about an old kiln over here somewhere," Shae interrupts the quiet. "It was used to store coal to feed the boiler and incinerators for the hospital. Now they just use it to make pottery and fire tiles to replace the crumbling ceiling. Art projects." She huffs with disapproval. "You say there isn't asbestos in this place, but have you seen the ceiling? It's falling apart. They're practically using slave labor to keep this place together."

I don't respond to her. Shae and I wander along the small, worn path as I consider how cogent she's been on this topic. Five minutes ago, she was practically catatonic, and now she's a whirl of opinions and concerns. People in her condition often swing from depressed to manic in a moment, but it's just not something I've seen from Shae before.

"I came back this morning to talk to you about something, Shae." A few more steps take place in silence. "I've been searching for a qualified therapist to take over your case, and I think I've found someone. They have experience working with clients who have been through—" I want to say the criminal justice system, but instead, I offer "—what *you've* been through."

Shae doesn't respond, but her steps slow a beat. We continue on until we come across a group of beehives that are buzzing with life. Shae pauses in front of the bees, watching them carefully. The silence is near deafening.

"Shae? Did you hear me?"

She doesn't respond. A prickle of fear runs up my spine. She seems disassociated, and nothing I can say will bring her back from wherever she is right now.

"Mia?" I utter, hoping to get her attention. A honeybee flies between us, breaking through the silence with its incessant buzz. It seems to be just enough to catch Shae's attention and hold it. She watches the bee for long moments before blinking and refocusing her dark eyes on mine.

Her stare turns accusatory. "You're leaving me?"

Chapter Forty-Two

Kelly Fraser, LLP

"I'm not leaving you. I'm searching for an alternative even better suited to help you during this time of your life." I pause. "I think you'll be in great hands."

"That sounds like bullshit."

"Shae—"

"Don't call me that." Shae walks off ahead of me on the trail. I rush to follow her as it curves around a broad evergreen. She's out of my sight, and I think for a moment this all might have been a mistake.

"Sorry. Mia! I'm sorry!" I call, speeding my steps until I'm breathing hard.

"You know what they're saying, don't you?" Shae halts, then turns to square off with me.

"Excuse me?" I stutter. Her eyes are dark and swirling with an emotion I can't quite place.

"Even if the judge says I'm guilty of taking people's money —I'm not because they *gave* it to me. I earned those donations because I entertained them. I gave them a little shot of dopamine in their newsfeed every day, and they gave me money in exchange. A tip, if you will. Some might call it performance art." She flips her wrist with a flourish. "They're all on my side, you know."

"*Who* is on your side?" My voice quivers.

"The internet. Who else, silly?"

"The internet?" I repeat, because surely I'm mishearing her. The way she's bouncing between topics makes me dizzy.

"The true crime forums, webzines, even some of the major news outlets are reporting on the #*TeamMia* hashtag that's trending on social media."

My mind blurs with questions. "But...what about the murder?"

"What murder?" Her gaze locks with mine. Something cold simmers in her irises.

"Jesika—the Riverwalk—there's security footage of the altercation between you."

"There was no altercation. She slipped and fell. You saw it on the video just like I watched it happen in person. I tried to save her life after she fell. You can see it on the footage. Any assumptions about anything else that led up to that point are just that—assumptions. You know what they say about assumptions, don't you, Kelly?" I shudder at the sound of my name on her lips. "Prosecutors spun a false narrative about a fight between us to try to convict me. Thankfully, it didn't work."

"Didn't it? You're here, aren't you?" I counter without thinking.

Shae's eyes flare with anger. She doesn't like being one-upped or outsmarted. It's the reason she can't get over Bishop flipping on her and why she could never get over her husband leaving her for another woman. Shae must be in complete control of her universe, and when she's not, she spirals into dangerous territory.

Is she exhibiting signs of psychosis? Maybe. It's hard to tell, and for the first time, I wonder if Shae is responding poorly to her meds—or if she's not taking them at all.

"The judge determined that I wouldn't be a good fit for prison. That sounds like a win to me." She almost seems to be gloating.

"Shae, the judge deemed you incompetent at the end of the trial, and instead of sentencing you, he committed you. It's hardly the upgrade you think it is."

Shae's eyes harden. "Obviously."

At that moment, it occurs to me that Shae is more cognizant of reality than she's been letting on.

"But...what about the baby?" I ask, desperate to distract her.

"What baby?" She chuckles in a way that turns my blood to ice. Shae rubs her tummy with both hands, then pinches at her muffin top. "I'm not pregnant. Just fat. Like *you*."

Hot tears sear my throat as I realize what's been happening all these months. Shae has been pretending to gain weight. Pretending to be pregnant. Pretending to be *crazy*.

Shae has been playing me. Shae has outsmarted all of us.

Chapter Forty-Three

Mia

"You know, Kelly." I circle my friend with a smile. "I've really been admiring this dress."

"W-what?" Her face crinkles in confusion.

I continue, enjoying toying with the woman who thought she was smarter than me. "Can I try it on?"

"No, of course not," Kelly spits, anger souring her sullen features. We were never friends; I know that now. I thought we were, but really, I knew that I was Kelly's pity friend, and I could only take it for so long. She chose me because she thought I didn't have anyone else. She chose me because it made her feel good to think she was helping an otherwise lost cause.

"Switch me." I seethe and use the razor-sharp tip of a small clay knife from the kiln to carve a line along her thigh.

"Shae—no. Stop." She turns, rearing one arm back like she's about to hit me with her tattered Louis Vuitton tote.

I'm ready for her, though. I've been waiting for this.

"You don't want to do that," I grit out, locking one of her wrists in my palm and spinning it behind her back. She's at my mercy now. The way I'm twisting her wrist is painful. Her soft, pillowy body is limp, but just to scare her, I drag the small, rusted hook on the end of the pottery knife along her cheek.

She's shaking and crying, her mascara is running, and something in me loves every moment of her misery.

I hook the dirty metal blade into her cheek and pull her skin taut. Tremors rack her body, and it feeds the power that's pumping through my blood.

"Switch. Me." I yank on the knife that's hooked in her mouth, and she screams.

"You're cutting me! Please! I can taste blood. You're cutting me." She's squirming against my hold. "Please don't hurt me."

"Switch clothes with me, or I'll cut you deeper." I pull again and notice a trickle of bright-red blood is sliding down her chin and neck. "I'm fat now. It should be just the right size."

Tears mix with blood from the inside of her cheek as she drops her bag and then loosens the tie on her wrap dress. She's sobbing now, but she's also stripping. I move quickly, keeping one eye on my friend as I shrug out of the oversized hospital gown.

"You could have gotten out early for good behavior, you know," Kelly snarls as she thrusts her dress at me.

"Shut up." I throw the gown at her, and she pulls it over her shoulders.

"You'll never get away with this." She is digging through her bag now.

"Give me that." I gesture to the bag. I know what she's up to —trying to locate her phone, probably.

"No," she growls.

"Don't. Tempt. Me." Before I can even finish putting on her wrap dress, I swipe at her with the pottery knife. I slash her cheek, and she cries out and holds a palm to her skin to stop the bleeding. "Hand over the Louis."

"*Fuck. You.*" Kelly's face is twisted with anger.

I laugh at the poor, pathetic woman in front of me. Hobbled on her knees, bloody and begging for my compassion. Just like Jesika. I blink away the flood of overwhelming emotion that threatens me.

"What did you think would happen?" I laugh. "You really thought we were just going to be friends? Best friends forever, like schoolgirls, huh?" I move closer, enjoying the way fear darkens her eyes. "We just needed matching necklaces. Speaking of—gimme that silver locket you're wearing too."

She blinks once, another burst of tears covering her cheeks. "From my sister? You monster."

An amused grin curves my lips. "I know you turned on me. I know about Tahoe."

"What do you mean?" She coughs out.

"Do you think I'm stupid? Do you really think I just went crazy? I know they had you wiretapped, I know they heard everything we talked about." My blood bubbles with anger the more I think about all this woman has put me through. "Just when I needed your help, you signed my death sentence." I hook the knife in her cheek again, dragging her to me. She howls with pain, and a fresh burst of blood covers her chin. "You tried to fuck me over, but I am *unfuckwithable*, bitch."

I cradle my round belly, rubbing it with my palm like a pregnant woman would. "I managed to trick them all. Do you really believe that I thought I was pregnant? I just needed you to think I believed it. It was fun, really, eating more cookies and acting like I was pregnant, trying to gain weight to look more like the woman who aided in my downfall."

Kelly slumps to the ground, her palm covering her mouth that's gushing crimson.

"Doesn't take much to put on fifty pounds, does it?" I trace the roundness of my belly with a fingertip. "Doesn't take much to make people think you're crazy either," I chuckle. "I just had to talk about choosing baby names now and again, and that was enough to convince the nurses I was insane. That was all it took to get them to ignore me. You know they never checked my room once to make sure I wasn't hiding my medication? Not once. What an oversight, don't you think?"

Moans interrupt my thoughts. It seems like she's trying to talk but can't. Only jumbled and garbled sounds are coming out. I blink, realizing what I've done. I've cut Kelly's tongue.

She can't talk.

My eyes cross the path and land on the small brick hut with a chimney billowing puffs of marshmallow-white smoke.

The kiln.

I swallow, realizing what I have to do. The path forward has been laid out before me for a reason. I have to do this. My survival depends on it.

"Come over here," I hiss, clasping her at the wrist and dragging her across the path. She doesn't fight me. I'm lucky. When I woke up today, I didn't realize it would be the day I've been waiting for, but opportunity has knocked, and I will answer it. Carpe *fucking* diem.

Once she's at the foot of the opening of the kiln, I pause and unlock the rudimentary sliding lock and swing the door wide. A wave of scorching heat washes over us and sends a thrill of anticipation through me.

"How lucky we are. It looks like someone is firing something pretty today." I heave her up against the flat stone step at the opening. "Up you go."

More garbled noises slice through the peace.

I regret the damage I've caused to her tongue, but it's another stroke of luck because it will be the catalyst that secures my freedom. I just have to ensure there's no chance she can heal enough to tell her story.

"Open up, babe." I speak like a doting mother trying to get a stubborn child to eat their peas.

Kelly doesn't respond. I spot a pair of rusted iron tongs used to move items in and out of the fire. I swipe them and gather a fiery orange coal in their grip. "Come on," I coo. "Be a good girl."

I grasp her face and force her mouth open. She doesn't have much fight left, but I persist. I have to make sure that when I leave here today, there are no witnesses who can speak to what happened.

My security requires her silence.

I think fast, wondering how I'll cover my tracks if I do this next part. I know I have mere minutes at most before someone realizes what's happened. I have to make the most of my next few steps. I bite down on my bottom lip; the taste of freedom is so sharp and sweet on my tongue I'm powerless to resist it. After being locked up in here for months, I'll do anything to escape.

"Don't make me mad." I push her mouth open wider and hover the coal at her lips. "Take it. Put it in your mouth and hold it there, bitch."

Tears blink from her eyes and mix with the blood that's drying on her cheeks.

"Do it. Don't make me mad." My threat finally lands because Kelly opens her mouth wider and leans in. She takes the coal in her mouth, and I turn away as the skin of her lips bubbles and peels. She howls like a wild animal, but before she can spit out the hot coal, I clamp a palm over her mouth and force her to hold it in.

"That's a good girl," I soothe. "The pain will be over soon."

Kelly begins to cough, I'm assuming, on the blood that must be choking her throat. Before this goes too far, I release her, allowing her to eject the hot coal from her mouth. It lands in the dirt and ash, no longer sizzling as the orange heat cools to a cloudy gray.

I can't think about the pain that must be piercing Kelly's system.

"This too shall pass." I move closer, inspecting her damaged form. "That's what my mother always said. You never know what you're made of until you walk through the fire." I chuckle softly at my unintentional pun.

I bend, clambering to control both of her flopping arms before I shove them fully into the fiery coals. She howls and writhes against me, but she's already in so much pain from the mouth injury she doesn't seem to have much control of herself. I don't want to end her life. I can't have that on my conscience. Though it might be easier on both of us if I did.

I only need to make sure she can't explain what happened today. She must be silenced forever. No words, no fingerprints, no way to communicate. No evidence of Kelly can remain.

The skin on Kelly's palms bubbles and blisters, the flesh raw and pink. It shines in an almost surreal way that reminds me of new-fallen snow or a sparkling morning dew. The sense of renewal and rebirth overwhelms me. Once I'm done here, we'll both have a chance at a fresh start.

My heartbeat roars in my ears as I hold her hands to the flames. I've done my best to mirror her as much as possible. It hurt me to gain nearly fifty pounds over the last six months—my streak of vanity runs far deeper than Kelly's.

"I would never be caught dead carrying that ugly old bag," I say aloud, unable to stop the wry cackle that leaves my lips. "Hopefully you don't have any fingerprints after this. We can't have anything that makes you identifiable as *Kelly Fraser, LLP,* now can we?"

I pull her palms from the hot coals, satisfied with the damage that's been done in just a few minutes.

"But what about that face?" I work my lips back and forth as I consider how to disfigure her just enough to disguise her true identity from the nurses. "Second-degree burns should be enough, right?"

A soft moan is my only reply before I heave her limp form up to the doorway again and then use her hand to swipe a pile of hot coals into her face. The skin on her cheeks sizzles and melts like bacon fat rendering in a skillet. I can't look any longer; it's an image that will take work to scrub from my brain.

"That should do the job." I turn, dropping my hold on her and smiling when the thud of her full weight hits the ground. "Now to leave a little goodbye note."

Digging through her dingy tote, I quickly find a pen and small pad of lined paper. Without thinking, I write out a quick suicide note.

I couldn't stay here any longer. I'm sorry for everything. xo Mia

I tear off the lined paper and fold it once before slipping it into the pocket of the blood-splattered hospital gown Kelly is wearing.

"*Sayonara,* bitch."

Chapter Forty-Four

I t takes me exactly three minutes from the moment I leave
Kelly at the kiln to the time I reach her small black
Nissan. I'm fighting to keep my wits about me as I navi-
gate the busy parking lot. After finding her keys in that filthy,
bottomless tote, I unlock the doors and then breathe a sigh of
relief when I slip behind the wheel.

The first thing I notice is an LA Dodgers baseball cap in the
back seat, so I push my hair into a ponytail and then pull the cap
low over my forehead. Smoothing the wrinkles in Kelly's dress, I
take a moment to really embody the energy of my friend.

I am Kelly Fraser, LLP now.

It's important I believe this if I'm going to keep up with this
new life. I've turned over a new leaf, and I've worked too hard to
jeopardize it now. I've risked too much to turn back. I've come
too far to only get this far. I take a few minutes to watch the
small groups of protestors and workers on strike that are
loitering around the entrance gates. I know that somewhere in
Kelly's bag, she'll have her hospital-issued identification card
that allows her entrance onto the grounds. I'm sure I'll be
checked on the way out of the gates, but with any luck, security

will be too busy trying to control the chaos of the crowd to be very thorough with checking me.

I shove both hands into Kelly's tote—*correction, my tote*—and dig through the junk until I find the badge and lanyard I'll need to get off the grounds. The picture on the front doesn't really look like me, but it doesn't really look like my therapist either. Her blond hair is the same—layered with feathered wisps along the fringe, but her face is thinner. I'd bet anything the photo is at least two decades old—maybe when she first received her therapy license from the state. It will have to work. I don't have a choice.

I stab the start engine button with my fingertip, relief flooding me as the car hums to life. I press my lips together, anxiety and anticipation mixing like a heady cocktail in my stomach. I take my time weaving through the groups of people, working my way closer and closer to the front gates. There are at least two dozen cars lined up along the road, some parked haphazardly in the ditch or with rear bumpers sticking into the traffic lane. It's absolute chaos, and it's the only way I can get away with what I'm about to do.

Shift change isn't for another hour, so I am the only car driving toward the gates that separate me from my freedom. The small security booth the guard sits in is crowded with people passing in and out. I have to wait for what looks like a local news crew to be admitted onto the grounds. Once they're allowed entrance, I creep the car up slowly and then idle at the open window.

I shove the lanyard with Kelly's identification out the window like I've done this a thousand times.

The guard greets me and reaches for the badge just as his phone rattles off the hook. He smiles easily, lifts a finger in indication that I wait a moment, and then answers the phone. "Guard shack."

My heart thunders as I pray it's not hospital staff calling to alert him to an escaped patient. I've been through a lockdown once before, when the schizophrenic down the hall from me went missing for a few hours. She was finally discovered by kitchen staff, hiding in the walk-in pantry, but until she was located, no person was allowed to leave the premises and all patients had to wait in their rooms. It was torture, but a valuable lesson in the preparedness of this place.

I wait patiently for the security guard to get off the phone. When he finally does, I hold my breath, expecting him to tell me he can't let me pass. Maybe I overlooked something—maybe there are security cameras posted around the grounds that I didn't account for. Maybe someone has already found Kelly bleeding out in the dirt and the hunt is already underway.

"Been a wild day, huh?" I attempt an awkward smile.

"Sure has, Miss Fraser. Did you enjoy your visit?" He only glances at my badge and then waves it away.

I glance at the name tag pinned to his uniform. "I always do, Theo."

The man smiles brightly, tipping his hat at me. "You have a nice day, now."

"You too," I call, waving as I ease away from the guard shack. One step away from incarceration and another step closer to freedom.

In that moment, my resolve crystallizes. My future beckons like the long, open road before me. Soon, I'll start over. Maybe Monterey or Mount Shasta. I think Kelly would flourish in a place like that. I smile, thinking of Kelly's admission that she'd found a new therapist for me—someone she thought would be a perfect fit. I sure hope it's as good a fit as Kelly believed, for her sake. I grin when I think of all the years of intensive psychiatric therapy and medications ahead of her. I marvel at the hours of careful planning that led up to this moment. From the day I was walked into the state hospital, I began planning my getaway.

More than just luck, it's a testament to my unshakable determination to persist through hardship. I am master of the pivot. Mia Starr will never be silenced; she's just on sabbatical for a while. I never allowed my mind to consider what I would do after my release from the state hospital. It felt like a dream too big to dream. Something far out of my reach. But as long as I can continue to make the most of each opportunity thrust my way, I know I can prevail. I will get my life back, and no one will stand in my way. Not Kelly or Jesika or Bishop. Not even the state of California.

I feel deliriously happy for the first time since I was pinned for the unfortunate accident that stole that woman's life on the Riverwalk. Friends or not, I resolve to leave the past in the past and never utter her name again. Vindication swells in my chest, and a smile so big it hurts my cheeks covers my face. Dean and I can get our lives back—maybe not now, maybe not soon. But we will. He is it for me. Even after all this time, I can feel him in my bones. He is part of me, and he always will be. I just have to make him see it too. And I know when the time is right, he'll be thrilled to see me.

I point my car in the direction of Chicago.

Fortune favors the bold, after all.

I just have to get rid of the blood on my hands first.

Epilogue

Kelly Fraser, LLP

"**S**he's still convulsing. Let's push another cc of anticonvulsant and see what happens."

My muscles twitch and pulse uncontrollably. The sensation of unfallen tears burning my eyelids is painful. I'd give anything to launch out of this bed and tell them they have the wrong person, but I can't.

Shae made sure of that.

I try again to moan, yell, form words at all, but I'm paralyzed from head to toe.

"I didn't know coma patients could have convulsions," the second nurse mumbles.

"Epileptic seizures are common after trauma, especially in the first seventy-two hours. It's less common a month on from the inciting event, but the surgeon thinks her body is reacting poorly to the skin grafts used to repair her tongue."

"Her tongue?" The second nurse sounds confused.

"Oh, I forgot that you weren't hired until after the strike..." The first nurse trails off. "Well, it was a crazy day. Shae left the hospital during the strike, and I think... Well, I think she thought she could get lost in the chaos and just...vanish." I can feel the

261

nurse pushing a fresh round of medicine into my IV. "They found her unconscious near the old kiln at the back of the property, third-degree burns covering her face and hands and a suicide note in her pocket. What a way to go, right? Death by fire. I think she had a psychotic break. She was so calm in the months leading up to that. I guess you never really know what's going on in someone's head, do you?"

More ravaged tears clutch at my throat. I never imagined I'd come to Pacific View Psychiatric and not leave. I never imagined that soon I would find myself trapped in my own body, unable to speak. Locked in a prison of singed flesh and excruciating pain. Frozen in flame forever.

And worse than the physical pain is the mental anguish of knowing that she will get away with it for one simple reason—no one knows to look for me. With my family gone and my sister living out her next adventure around the globe, there hasn't been anyone to worry about me in a long time. I mentioned moving the last time I spoke to my sister, so even when she comes home someday, she won't know where to look. I came into this world alone, and I will die alone. I've tried to resolve myself to this thought over the last month, but on good days...on good days, I allow myself to dream of a time when I'm healed. If I could only form enough words to ask for a DNA test, I could prove I am not who they think I am. I could prove that I was framed. I could prove that the real villain didn't attempt suicide that day; she got away.

I realize now she asked so many questions about my family not because she wanted to get to know me, but because she was gathering information. Every moment of our time together was a fact-finding mission, the knowledge stored away in her mind until it was of use to her. Just when I thought I'd finally found a true friend.

Some people leave a mark on you, and you have to live with the scar.

A phantom shudder racks my body as I focus all of my concentration on forming my lips into a single word: *Shae.*

THE END

Shae's story continues in The Imposter.

Do you love to read?

Sign up for **New Release Alerts** from Adriane here.
https://adrianeleigh.myflodesk.com/booknews

Are you a book reviewer that loves to read psychological thrillers?

Join my review team
and get copies of my new releases
before they publish:
https://www.adrianeleigh.com/reviews

Acknowledgments

I am so grateful for the constant support and cheerleading from so many.

This story wouldn't be what it is without my dear friend, Nelle Lamarr. Every moment we share is inspiring. Thank you for being so open and honest and fabulously you!

Thank you to Lisa at Silently Correcting Your Grammar for delving deep inside Shae's crazy mind with me!

To my family—I couldn't do this job without your love lifting me. You're crazy and funny and basically my favorite humans. Thank you for being you and allowing me to be me.

And to the readers. I've been publishing for 12 years and what a ride it's been! Thank you for taking this word journey with me. I am so humbled and honored by you. *xxx A*

Also by Adriane Leigh

"Fans of Riley Sager will love The Last Writer. An addictive, bone-chilling book! Be sure to keep the lights on!" - Nelle L'Amour, New York Times Bestselling Author of That Man

The Cowboy's Claim

Stolen by the Mountain Man

...and many more, all available in KindleUnlimited!

**Sign up for new release alerts at
https://www.adrianeleigh.com**

About the Author

Adriane Leigh is a USA Today bestselling author of multiple novels and novellas. With appearances in publications such as Vogue Magazine and The Montreal Gazette, the award-winning author, in addition to writing, founded RARE: Romance Author & Reader Events, a community of internationally-renowned book conventions that draw thousands of readers and #1 bestselling authors to events around the world each year.

She hosts a podcast, The Rebel Artist, and her books are translated into French, Spanish, Italian, and Portuguese.

She lives on Lake Michigan with her family.

Visit adrianeleigh.com for events, new releases, and more.